THE MAGIC MAKER

THE MAGIC MAKER

JOYCE VARNEY

Illustrated by Trina Schart Hyman

The Bobbs-Merrill Company, Inc.
A Subsidiary of Howard W. Sams & Co., Inc.

PUBLISHERS • INDIANAPOLIS • KANSAS CITY • NEW YORK

To all my favorite children,
and especially to John Green, Michael Bisbee,
Jamey Malin and Christopher Martin Blair

THE MAGIC MAKER

1

CLANG! went the school bell, bringing Twm Tybach (Toom TUH-bock) upright. He had been hunting for a cuckoo among the wild wet bluebells. Now he hopped like a cricket on a hot stone and started to run. But in the distance he could see that the schoolyard was empty. No use hurrying now.

The damage was done. He was late and in trouble again. Twm didn't mean to, but he was always making trouble. Only this morning he had forgotten and let the speckled hens out of their pens, and they had gone through Gran's London Prides. Then he had banged the door so hard that the bread fell. And now he was late for school again.

Miss Davies would say: "Late again, late again." She repeated herself, always. She had warned him that she would give his part as king of the tegs in the pageant to Gerwin Thomas, who was never late. And she might send Twm to the headmaster for the cane.

The schoolyard was chapel quiet. Twm crept in the door and into the classroom, not daring to look towards her desk, but waiting for Miss Davies to spring at him like a cat. But it was another voice that said:

"You are late."

Twm's eyes opened wide in surprise. Behind Miss Davies's desk stood a pretty lady with hair as fair as Twm's. It brought to his mind all the stories his Gran had told him about the tylwyth teg, the white witch, that fair and terrible flying creature who lived in damp bogs and places dark with trees. Where did this one come from, Twm wondered. She didn't speak like anyone in the valley, but like people in American movies.

"Sit down," the lady said firmly. "I will talk to you later."

She was a teacher all right, and her name was Miss Olson. It was written on the blackboard.

"Today," she continued, "I will tell you something about America, and perhaps you will then tell me something about Wales."

Smiles and murmurs ran through the class.

"No sums?" whispered Mortimer Weeks, who sat on one side of Twm and who was Twm's second-best friend.

"I hope she stays," said his best friend Gypsy, who sat on the other.

" 'Course she will stay," said Mortimer sharply.

Twm was too interested in what the American teacher was

saying to listen to them. He leaned forward and strained so not to miss a word. His mouth watered when she told about the twenty-eight flavors of ice cream they made in America. She said that in Detroit they turned out mile after mile of shining new cars, all colors. Then she spoke about the shoes they made in New England, the pins in Connecticut, and the clocks and watches they made in Massachusetts. Millions of them. One clock should last a lifetime, Twm thought. At his house they were still using the one that belonged to his great-great-grandfather. How careless they must be in America.

Clang! went the school bell. The morning had gone faster than the wink of a cat's eye. Now I can have fun with Gypsy, Twm thought happily. He grinned at Gypsy, and Gypsy grinned back in anticipation.

Suddenly the classroom door opened and the headmaster came striding in. Pin-drop silence greeted him. Twm and Gypsy exchanged furtive glances. Which one of them would it be? Twm hadn't skipped school this month. Still, he had been late. As the master talked quietly to Miss Olson, his little black eyes swept around the room. They rested on Twm, and seemed to unbutton all his thoughts. His pulse stood still as he gazed with respect on the thin cane that the master held in his large hairy hand. And Twm's face lit up with a glow of gratitude and prayer when the tiny eyes passed over him.

But Gypsy, who had been suffering just as hard, wasn't so

lucky. The master pointed to him and Gypsy stood up. His face was soaked in misery for a second, but then there was the old fire in his eyes. Gypsy was always in trouble at home and school. He was wild and lawless, people in the valley said. And he had mitched school five times this month. Twm played with him every time he got the chance. And it was almost worth the cane to mitch school with Gypsy, because he could fight harder, climb trees higher, and spit farther than anybody. And Gypsy knew all the secret places in the woods where the lark, the swallow and the white-breasted thrush nested. Twm decided to give Gypsy his garter snake. That would take his mind off his troubles. No, Gypsy wasn't a babby. He would simply cool his hurt hands on the wet grass, and then he and Twm could have fun.

Twm was rising from his desk to go out into the school-yard, and about to take his hot potato off the potbellied stove, when Miss Olson said: "I want to see you, Twm Tybach."

"Oh, no," thought Twm. "Now I will have it for sure."

"Why were you late, Twm?"

He hung his head. Sometimes this worked with Miss Davies.

The lady bent down until her face was level with his. Her hair was really soft and warm, the color of wheat now. He dared to touch it. She turned quickly.

Twm hung his head again.

"Look at me, Twm," she said.

"Yes, miss." She was smiling. There's a surprise. Her teeth were glistening white, like the beads Mam wore to chapel.

The smile made him brave. "Your hair, miss. It's the color of mine."

"Is that so unusual?"

She must be dense, thought Twm. Anyone in Wales knows that blond hair means trouble. She must have heard about Welsh tegs—everybody knew about them. "Look one in the eye on Sunday and your eyes will cross on Monday." That was why most of the children in class wouldn't sit next to Twm.

"Will you answer me?" asked the teacher. "I want to know why you are always late."

"My gran says it is because, because I'm part teg, mun," he explained. "I belong to the witches who have white hair," said Twm, tactfully avoiding her eye or adding, white like yours, miss. Twm's statement seemed to have a terrible effect on the teacher. She went bright pink and held her handkerchief to her mouth. There's guilty, Twm thought.

"Tell me more about these tegs," said the teacher, recovering herself.

"Related to the white witches, they are. Tegs can fly around the moon," he whispered. "You can sometimes see them on a misty night."

"You have seen them?"

Twm looked around to be sure that no one was listening. "I'm sure I did once," he whispered. "They be crafty, see, and bad."

"What do they do that's bad?"

"They make people dance in their magic ring."

"Is that so bad?"

"A miner coming out of the coal pits after working all day does not feel like dancing, miss."

"You wouldn't do that, would you, Twm?" asked the teacher. "You wouldn't make them dance?"

"No," said Twm readily. Then he added in a burst of confidence, "But I'd make Miss Davies dance."

"Twm, why?"

Twm pondered. Better not say why. Once he started on Miss Davies he would have to go on and on, telling how ugly she was with that big brown wart on her chin with hair sprouting from it and about her saying everything twice.

"Anyway, I'm only part teg," he said changing the subject.

"Oh, how do you know?"

"Because I can't fly."

"You have tried?"

"Aye, and I fell on my nose."

"I suppose that settles it," she said.

Twm searched her face. But it was sober as Sunday.

"Twm, I understand you have a good singing voice."

Ha! How did she know?

"Twm?"

"Aye, miss, I sing fair to middling." Then his face brightened. "I'm going to be king of the tegs in the Whitsuntide pageant."

"Not if you play hooky any more."

"Hooky?"

"Yes, skipping school."

"Oh gee, miss, I only mitched twice last month, and none this month," said Twm, stung.

"Twice after you were warned by Miss Davies."

Twm hung his head. He had talked too much.

"The town has a big festival every year, doesn't it, Twm?"

"Aye," breathed Twm, "and the pageant is part of it, see. This year our school is going to do the Druids."

"Indeed?"

"Aye, they were wild men who used to live here, see. They worshiped the sun and ran around with holly in their hair and cut the mistletoe with a golden knife." He stopped for a breath. "They had tegs too, mind, in those times. And my gran says we still have them."

"You like the festival, Twm?"

"Aye, mun. It is the best time of the year. All the valley goes, see. Proud Parry opens up his land to everybody. A bard is crowned for the best song. My dada might get it this time. And we sing and everything." Twm's eyes grew brighter. "You should see it, miss. There's Gypsy carnivals with big tents that light up the night. That's the night Gypsy always looks for his tribe," he whispered. "Then there are hurdy-gurdies, swing boats and roundabouts. And then the contest of the pageants, and songs. My dada is sure to win this time."

"It sounds like fun."

"Aye, mun. We have apples and oranges, Welsh taffy, and currant cakes by the cartload."

"Yes, it sounds like fun. Twm, why are you always late?" she asked suddenly.

Why did she have to start that again, Twm thought. He turned his head.

"And why don't you like school, Twm?"

Hah, she knew that, too. He shuffled his feet and kept his eyes on the floor.

"Twm, I'm waiting."

He shoved his hands deep into his pockets. She wasn't going to get any more news out of him, not if he could help it.

"Twm," she demanded. "Answer me."

"I don't like school because it takes too much time," he muttered.

"But you liked it this morning."

"Aye, I liked it this morning all right."

"What would you rather do with your time?"

"I'd rather go into the woods," he burst out.

"I can understand that, Twm. But you have plenty of time after school for that."

"The morning is the best time to catch the cuckoo."

"Then you are going to have to catch him on Saturday, Twm. I'll tell you a secret. If you paid more attention in school you might find out a lot more about the cuckoo. Men who have loved birds as much as you have made a study of them."

"I bet I know more than they do."

"Well, let's get some books about birds and find out, shall we?"

"Aye, yes, miss."

"And let's not be late any more, Twm?"

Asking him . . . not telling him like old Miss Davies.

"You will remember, Twm?"

"Yes, miss. Indeed to goodness I will."

"Right then. Be back by the bell."

She is no teacher, Twm decided. She is a teg. A nice friendly one, I hope. He hopped out of the school chanting: "Look a teg in the eye on Sunday; go cockeyed on Monday."

2

"If you ask me, that new teacher is barmy," Mortimer was saying to Willy. "Isn't that right, Twm?" he shouted. "Isn't that teacher barmy and simple, and she be blond as well?"

Twm tried to change the subject. "Has Gypsy come out of the headmaster's office yet?"

"No," said Willy, "and he will be sent to reform school for sure. My mam says it's a disgrace that they haven't done something about him before now. Always mitching school and running away."

Gerwin joined the group. "He's a terrible boy. My mam says."

"He is not," Twm replied.

"I said that teacher be barmy," said Mortimer, angry because Gerwin and Twm were talking about something else. "She be. She be barmy and she be simple, too." And Mortimer laughed. He could never laugh without hitting someone and he hit Twm good-naturedly.

Twm hit back good-naturedly. "She is not barmy," he said.

"Well then, what is she?" demanded Mortimer, his eyes growing dark gray. "Suppose you tell me what she is—a teacher who gives no sums, no spelling. I say she be barmy." And he brought his face so close Twm could count the freckles. Mortimer's red hair stood up like a flame of a candle. "All right. You tell me what she is."

"Well," muttered Twm. "Well . . ."

"What is she?" shouted Mortimer.

"Give me a chance, mun. Well, she's . . ." Twm caught himself in time. He was about to say that she was a teg. Better not. "She's an American. That's what she is. An American teacher. How would you like to be called barmy and simple just 'cause you came from America, mun?"

"Indeed to goodness," taunted Mortimer. "Twm Tybach has turned into a teacher's babby."

"I'm not. I'm not," cried Twm hotly, and he pushed Mortimer. And then the fight was on.

"Hit him! Hit him!" called Willy Burton. "Hit the teacher's babby. Hit him in the nose, hit him in the bread-basket." Willy shadowboxed around the fighting boys, and when Willy got excited, one of his eyes crossed. He squinted through his fingers, and continued to dance around and chant: "Hit him! Hit him!"

"What's going on?" other boys wanted to know.

Willy stopped long enough to consider. "They be fighting," he said finally.

"I can see that, dull," said Jethro Roberts scornfully, pointing his long nose at Willy. "What be they fighting about?"

"Twm is a teacher's babby," said Willy promptly.

"I always knew it," said Gerwin delightedly, and he joined in the chant: "Teacher's babby. Teacher's babby," for Twm had often called him by that name.

And soon a crowd of boys gathered like bees around honey. Twm was holding his own very nicely, mind, until Willy pinched him. He let out a howl, and when he was off guard, Mortimer punched him in the eye.

"I saw that. I saw that," said Gypsy running up to where Twm stood holding his eye. "Right then, Willy, how about a round with me?"

Soon Gypsy and Willy, and Twm and Mortimer were going at it hot and heavy. When Twm wasn't looking, Gerwin pinched his potato from his back pocket. "Hey," Twm protested, and Mortimer popped Twm in the other eye. Twm reeled among exploding stars.

"Come on, Twm," urged Gypsy. He had soon polished

off Willy, who was now sniffling quietly in the corner. "Come on, Twm."

Suddenly there was a cry: "Here comes teacher. Here comes teacher." All the boys stood as though turned to stone.

"What is this?" demanded Miss Olson.

No one answered.

"Twm," she asked, "what is this?"

"Nothing, miss," Twm replied through a thick lip.

"Nothing, Twm?"

Twm prayed that she would do or say nothing that would convince the boys that he was a teacher's babby.

"Your eye is closing," she said, taking out a handkerchief and gently wiping his face. Twm wished the ground would open up and swallow him. He heard titters. "Did you do this?" she demanded of Mortimer.

"Aye, miss," he replied proudly.

"You little bully. Now say you are sorry."

"Sorry," blurted Mortimer looking at Twm.

"I started it, miss," said Twm fearing that she would go over his face with the handkerchief again.

"Why?"

"I just did," said Twm desperately.

"Then I'm disappointed in you." And much to Twm's horror she wiped his face with the handkerchief again.

"Please, miss, I'm all right," Twm pleaded.

Miss Olson regarded him with eyes as calm and blue as

willow plate. She smiled gently and patted Twm on the head and he wished he could die. Now the other boys nudged each other. Miss Olson looked from Twm to them.

"Well," she said briskly, "don't do it again, Twm Tybach. And Mortimer, now I know you have so much energy I'd like to see more of it in the classroom."

Mortimer scowled.

She smiled at all of them before she turned away, and as soon as she was out of earshot, Mortimer said: "She be not a bad teacher."

"Now, who's being a teacher's babby?" shouted Twm. "Now who?" and the fight started again.

Twm was so tired he was getting the worst of it. Mortimer stood back with his fist raised. "All right," he said, "am I best fighter?"

"No," said Twm weakly.

"Right then," cried Mortimer finishing Twm off with a punch in the nose.

"Look at him bleed," cried Willy, and several girls scattered like mice when they saw the blood on Twm's face.

"I can fight you, too, Twm Tybach," squeaked Gerwin, who never fought anyone.

"Aye," said Gypsy scornfully, "easy to fight a boy with two black eyes and a busted nose. Come and try me, Gerwin."

"You stay away from me," cried Gerwin. "My mother said I mustn't have anything to do with you. You be Gypsy blood." And that was all for Gerwin, who felt Gypsy's fist on the end of his nose. Mortimer looked at Gypsy cautiously and laughed hollow as a coffin. "I don't mind playing with you, Gypsy. In fact, we are going to start a new secret society. You can join."

"I don't mind," said Gypsy; then he saw Twm's reproachful stare. "That is, if Twm joins."

"Aw, we don't want a teacher's babby, mun," Mortimer said. "He will just blab anything."

"No, indeed to goodness he won't," said Gypsy loyally.

"Yes, he will blab."

Twm never knew how he did it but all at once he was on top of Mortimer punching and hitting in blue rage, while all the boys that stood around were now shouting for Twm. And then Twm went for Gerwin and the boys shouted louder like it was judgment day.

"Where is my potato?" demanded Twm.

"Willy took it," cried Gerwin in terror. "Willy took it. I wasn't going to eat it, honest."

"Where is it, Willy?"

"I ate it. I ate it. You can't have it back 'cause I ate it."

Twm shook Willy with what strength he had left. An apple rolled out of Willy's pocket. Twm bit into it with his sharp white teeth, although he wasn't hungry any more. He felt sick and tired and longed to lie down. This is what happened when you got mixed up with a real teg. His clothes were torn, his eyes were smarting, his nose was throbbing. He had lost his second best friend and his hot potato. Not that he cared about Mortimer, mind. But they called him a teacher's babby. The worst name in the world. She will never cast her magic on me again, vowed Twm.

"Come over by here, Twm," Gypsy said. "Hold your head back to stop your nose bleeding."

Twm stumbled over against the wall, and soon Gypsy was telling him about the awful caning he had gotten from the master.

"I'm going to run away where they will never find me."

But Twm wasn't even listening. For the first time in his life he was grateful the school bell rang. Now at least he could go in and sit down. But he was going to watch out for that teg.

For the rest of the afternoon, Twm did all he could to avoid hearing Miss Olson. He stuffed his ears with blotting paper and tried thinking about the dingle.

But the teg's words kept creeping in. Twm could see the valley where gold was found, where trees seemed to brush the sky, trees so big around that men cut tunnels through them for shiny new cars to go through. He was completely lost in her words.

"I have been talking all day," Miss Olson said. "Now I want you to tell me something about Wales."

"I know the longest word in the world," said Twm throwing caution to the wind.

"Yes," said Miss Olson eagerly.

"It is LLANFAIRPWILLGWYNGLLGOGERYCHYRNDROBWILL-ANTSYSILIOGOGOGOCH."

"Wow!" said Miss Olson. "What does it mean?"

"I know," said Mortimer bursting with information. "It means the church of St. Mary in a hollow of white hazel, near a rapid whirlpool, and near a red cave." He stopped for breath.

"But the people just call it LLANFAIRPWILL," said Twm glaring at Mortimer.

"I should hope so," said Miss Olson. "It would be hard to get all that on an envelope. Now what else can you tell me?"

The bell sounded again. The morning had gone fast, but the afternoon faster.

"Twm," said Miss Olson, "I'd like to see you before you go."

"Yes, miss," Twm sighed.

"Run along, Mortimer," she added, for Mortimer was hanging around fishing in his desk. He smirked at Twm before going out the door. Oh, why doesn't she leave me be? Twm wondered. He had enough for one day.

"Feel better, Twm?"

"I'm all right, miss."

"You fight often?"

"No, miss."

"Why did you fight today?"

"I started it," said Twm.

"So you said. Was it because of me?"

She was a teg and no mistake.

"Twm," she said gently, "you write very nice poetry."

Twm gasped. How did she know?

"I love the woods too, Twm," she confided.

"You do?"

"Sometime I will tell you how my brother and I spent a long time in the woods. We lived there and everything. We caught our food, and we slept in a hollow tree."

Twm was dying to ask if they flew as well, and was about to when she become all brisk again.

"Now, Twm, there is no excuse for your getting these low marks. You have a brain. I want you to use it. I will help you if you will let me."

"Help me get good marks? That would please Mam and Dad."

"Well then, let us work hard together. I can teach you many things."

Aye, I bet you can, Twm thought. But would she teach him what he wanted to learn most, to fly? "I'll show you the dingle if you like," he said, before he could stop himself. What would Gypsy and Mortimer say? Showing a teacher their secret place. They would surely call him a teacher's babby.

"Why Twm, I would like that."

"Perhaps you wouldn't," he said. "Girls don't."

"But Twm, I love the woods. You could show me things, and I could . . ."

"Right then, Saturday it is. That's if it doesn't rain."

"Well, all right, Twm. Saturday it is, if it doesn't rain."

3

Twm walked home in such deep thought that he hardly heard Gypsy.

"You be listening to me," Gypsy finally said. "I said I'm going to run away."

"Don't be daft, Gypsy," Twm answered. "They will only find you again and bring you back. They always do. The widow greengrocer adopted you, mun. You have got to stay."

Gypsy's eyes became all mystery and brightness. "I'm only staying until I find my tribe. Then I will go off with them and live in a caravan."

"Aye," said Twm absently. "Gypsy, do you believe in magic?"

"Aye, Gypsy magic."

"No, I mean Welsh magic . . . tegs."

"Aye."

"Can you fly?"

"No, can you?"

"I can't say yet. Gypsy, how be you magic?"

Gypsy grinned. "When I run away from the widow no one can find me."

"Hey, Gypsy, there's the widow waiting for you at the door of the greengrocer shop. See you tomorrow."

Twm started to run towards his house. What a strange day it had been. No sums, no spelling, nothing to do but enjoy yourself. What a strange people Americans were, and what a wonderful country it must be.

"Yes indeed," said Twm's grancher later when Twm breathlessly told him about the teacher and America. "That would be a wonderful place to go and be a singer. You have been practicing, boy, bach?"

"Aye, Grancher. Do you know that in America they make enough thread in one mill to go around the world? Imagine that? Around the world. Gran could never do that on her spinning wheel."

"Goodness, what did you do to your eye?" asked Mam. "Twm, you have been fighting again. Wait until your father comes home," she stormed.

"Sorry, Mam."

"Look at your trews. Do you think the money for new ones grows on trees?" And she plunged her hands into the bread she was mixing, working it fiercely as though to punish it for the shortcomings of Twm.

"And now you just listen to me, Twm," she went on. "It's high time you stop your fighting ways and pay attention to your schooling. Nine is old enough to take some responsibility, and you will be ten soon. Morfydd does not give me this trouble," she added darkly, spooning the mixture into the tins.

Twm said nothing. Morfydd could do no wrong. She was his twin, and different from Twm as chalk from cheese. Twm was glad he wasn't like her. A boy would be daft to want to be like Morfydd. They had started school together in the infants' class, but Morfydd had been too clever to stay there long. Indeed, she was so smart she made Twm and the rest of the class uneasy. They were all glad to get rid of her when she skipped a grade. She was dark as Twm was fair. Sitting prim in her pinafore, studying, asking the teacher to bring her fresh books, showing off her pencils that always needed sharpening because she worked so hard—she was a freak, Twm decided. Thank goodness she had skipped to the big room, no doubt making everyone uncomfortable there.

Twm's mam sighed and Twm was thankful her anger was gone. Perhaps if he was lucky it would be forgotten before Dada came home. But what Twm needed now more than anything was to talk to Gran.

Gran was in the little room behind the kitchen where she

tapped and mended the boots. Twm quietly went in and made himself useful by sorting out the leather and hobnails.

"Let me look at your boots," said Gran, and Twm obediently lifted up his boot.

"He makes sparks up the hill with them," said Morfydd coming in and looking as cool and neat as a new pin.

"All you can expect from a half teg," said Gran darkly. "The dancing teg."

"No indeed," called Grancher from the kitchen, "tegs are supposed to be light on their feet."

"What is all this about tegs?" called Twm's mam. "Stop filling him full of that nonsense. Tegs indeed."

"You all make fun of what you do not understand," said Gran, "but I know well about tegs and their mischief."

Twm prayed that Morfydd would go. He wanted so to talk with Gran, but Morfydd just stayed and stayed.

"A new teacher in Twm's class," she chanted. "Blond as milk."

"Diawl!" said Gran. "Another teg is it?"

"No, American," Twm answered hotly.

"Exchange teacher," Morfydd corrected. "She flew across the ocean."

"Never!" said Twm.

"She did, too," replied Morfydd. "She came over on a plane. Mr. Roberts told us so, so there." She poked her tongue out at Twm and went off outside.

Twm breathed a sigh of relief. Trouble Miss Olson would have if the valley people thought she could fly, but it irritated Twm that Morfydd, as usual, knew more about how the teacher came than he did. He wanted to give her a shove.

"Gran," Twm said after Morfydd had gone, "tell me again why I'm part teg?"

Gran began to sort the nails. "You know as well as I do." She looked at him over the full moons of her steel-rimmed glasses.

"Tell me again, Gran, please."

"Well, what do they like to eat?"

"Hedge leaf," said Twm promptly.

"And what else?"

"Toasted cheese."

"And you?"

"I like the same things exactly. Same, same exactly," said Twm.

"How do they sing?"

"High and sweet," Twm replied, "but no one can ever remember their tune."

"And you sing almost as sweet as your grancher did at your age," Gran said dreamily.

"Is Grancher part teg?"

"Watch your words," Gran said sharply. "You know many is the time I have heard the tegs around Proud Parry's land. When I was a girl, that is. Lucky for me there was always water between me and them, so they never enchanted me."

"What else, Gran?"

She pointed to Twm. "They have small ears, pointed at the top like yours, and they are quick like a swift bird. They do awful mischief like somebody I could mention."

"Dada is home," called Morfydd at Twm as she came running in the house. "I saw him at the bottom of the street. Now you will have it, boyo."

As she spoke Twm heard his father's footsteps in the passageway, and heard his mother say: "Hywel, please will you talk to that boy of yours. He came home again with his trews all ripped and his eye black. A regular tough he is getting."

"Aye, just give me time to get in, Tessa love," he said. "Twm," he called.

Twm glanced quickly at his father. He didn't seem upset yet. Perhaps he had a poem in his head. His father spent half of his time in a world of his own where Mam's ups and downs passed practically unnoticed.

"I don't know where it's all going to end," continued his mam. "Probably in the coal mines."

This brought his father up sharp. He peered at Twm, his big blue eyes glistening in the black face, his scarlet mouth going thin.

"Fighting again is it, boy?" he asked quietly.

"Aye, Dada."

"Twm!" he thundered. "How many times have I told you that I won't have a fighter in this house?"

"He fights all the time, Dada," said Morfydd.

"Heisht, Morfydd. Well, Twm?"

"I didn't start it," said Twm. "Mortimer called me a teacher's babby because I wouldn't agree with him that the American teacher was barmy."

His dada studied Twm for a moment. "Right you were, my son," he said. "But did you need to fight? Isn't it enough for you to know that you are not a teacher's babby?"

"There were other boys around."

"So you had to convince them, eh? Do you think you did?" asked his father.

"I knocked Mortimer down."

"And what did that do?"

"He won't call me teacher's babby again."

"True, true," said his father. "Well what is for supper, Tessa?"

"What about those trews?" demanded Twm's mother.

"Aye," said his father. "You know the rules, Twm. Ripped trews and you get punished."

"Even if I didn't start the fight?"

"Even so, I have to buy new thread to sew your trews, Twm. But I will let you off with a warning this time."

"He was late for school again," said Morfydd.

"That settles it then," said his father in a quiet angry voice. "Into the shed, boyo."

Morfydd started to cry. Just like her, thought Twm. Get you into trouble one minute and cry basinsful the next.

Dada's words hurt Twm far more than the beating. "Twm," he said sadly, "you must do better than this. You promised only yesterday that you wouldn't be late for school again."

"I will do better . . . I will," Twm said almost crying. Although Dada rarely raised his voice like Mam, his worried look and scoldings shamed him. But why was school so important to Dada? Hadn't he left school at fourteen to go into the coal mines? And Twm wanted to do just what Dada had done. He wanted to come home with a blackened face and glistening white eyeballs. He wanted his hobnail boots to spark up the hill, and he wanted to have a tin water bottle and wear a flame on his miner's hat.

Twm sat quietly eating his supper. It was good broth made out of sheep's head. There was parsley and wild onions in it, and marigold from Gran's garden. Dessert was rice pudding and tinker's cake bursting with currants. But Twm ate little and wished for a smile and a word that everything was right again. Instead Dada ordered Twm to bed early.

"But he must practice tonight for the pageant," said Grancher. "Whitsuntide is only two weeks away."

Twm went quickly up the stairs just in case his sister,

Morfydd, had heard and would tell that Twm would lose his part in the pageant if he was late to school many more times. Twm listened at the stairs. No, she didn't say anything. But Grancher kept on about his singing.

"He shouldn't play so much with that Gypsy boy," said Gran. "Nothing but a little poacher is that tramping boy, Gypsy."

"Mother, please," said Dada. "He is an orphan, poor boy."

"A ragged heathen," said Gran. "A wild Gypsy. Always running away and making his bed under the moon like his caravan kin. Poor widow greengrocer has tried to make a Christian out of him, but it's a losing battle."

"Heisht, Mother," said Grancher. "He and Twm have been friends for a long time. Old friends are better than new."

"Well I hope the beating did some good," said Mam.

"I hope so, Tessa girl," replied Dada. "I want something better for my son than crawling underground like an ant."

"He'll be a fine singer, never fear," said Grancher. "Don't worry, Hywel boy."

"But I do worry, Dad," said Twm's father to Grancher. "The coal mines are full of singers and poets all lacking the learning to escape."

"You are tired," said Twm's mam. "Come, Hywel, and I will play the harp and sing to you. Your new poem, is it? The one that is sure to win at the festival?"

Twm trudged sadly into his room. He heard his mother's

deep voice floating up, singing the words of his father's poem. No one could make songs like Dada. Wonderful words that made Twm's stomach throb, that made him sad and happy at the same time. Please, let Dada be crowned bard at the festival . . .

He listened until the new moon came over the mountain, moon enough to light up the brass knobs of his bed.

Now Twm had to face something else that he had been pushing to the back of his mind. He had told the teg he would take her to the dingle on Saturday. Twm decided he had better pay special attention to his prayers. He kneeled down on the floor and, tucking his nightshirt around his feet, he prepared himself for a long conversation with God.

After "Gentle Jesus, meek and mild," he made up a prayer of his own. "Don't let it come out about the teacher and the dingle. The boys would laugh at me, see, and never stop calling me teacher's babby. No, you wouldn't let it come out, would you? I'll try and do what Dada wants. And please let him win the prize. But oh, baby Jesus, please ask your big father, God, to keep it quiet. And I'll never be bad again, honest. Amen."

Twm scrambled into bed among the duck feathers. He pulled the Welsh flannel blankets over his head to keep out the wicked thoughts that sometimes came to him. He had great faith in Jesus, mind, and felt better after his prayers.

4

BY THE NEXT MORNING Twm had made up his mind that there was no sense worrying about something that might never happen. Saturday was at least three days away and that was ages. It might thunder or rain, or Miss Olson might take it into her head not to go to the dingle.

He came whistling down the stairs to breakfast.

"Lovely day, Grancher," he said. "It was so warm in the night, I kept my window open."

This brought Grancher up from his morning paper. "Twm boy, you didn't catch cold?" he asked anxiously. "You never can tell what the night air will do to the throat."

"Never mind his throat," said Twm's mam with a grin. "Look at that neck. Under the tap before breakfast," she ordered, as Twm was about to sit down to a steaming bowl of gruel and brown sugar. "The tide mark is up to your ears," she scolded, "and your nails are deep in mourning."

"And when you go back to the pump," said Gran, "don't you dare let those hens out again."

Twm trudged out the back to the pump thinking that all the pepper in the house was not on the spice shelf. He hopped as the water came out of the pump in cold blue gulps. He gasped as he stuck two fingers under it and cat-licked his face.

"Comb your hair, too," called Mam. So Twm pulled the gap-toothed comb through his tangled hair and thought again how much easier the world would be if women were not forever worrying about dirt.

But they don't mean harm, he thought, as he watched Gran take the golden, sizzling Welsh cakes from the griddle and put them into a snowy towel to keep warm. If Gran gave him two, Twm decided to give one to Miss Olson.

"See what it says right here in the paper," said Grancher excitedly. "Auditions for the Christmas pantomime will be held by David Lewis in the town hall Wednesday. That's today. From nine A.M. to three. Twm, I think you should go. They are going to do *Babes in the Wood* this year, mun."

"Isn't he too big for the Babe?" said Morfydd coming in prim as a lady lark, her hair ribboned, her face shining.

"No, indeed," said Grancher. "He is small for his age. Pity he wasn't old enough last year when they put on *Jack and the Beanstalk.*"

"Well, I think he is too big for the Babe," said Gran. "He'll never get the part."

"You know," said Grancher, paying no attention, "Twm should go and audition right now. What is one day of school?"

Twm glanced at his father to see how he was taking it. But he went on mending his tin water bottle with a tinker's patch, lost in a dream and not hearing even a word.

"Hywel," said Twm's mam, "don't you hear what is going on? Grancher wants Twm to skip school for this audition. It would be one thing if there were a chance of his getting it, but . . ."

"Of course he will get it," interrupted Grancher stoutly.

"School is more important than anything," said Twm's father. "Tessa, I have been thinking . . . that new teacher must be lonely, so far away from home. We must ask her to tea."

"Oh, Hywel, with this houseful?"

"Yes, Tessa. It is the least we can do seeing she has come so far."

"It will mean opening up the parlor," said Mam doubtfully.

"She couldn't come anyway," said Twm. "She's awfully busy."

"How do you know?" asked Morfydd, who liked to have teachers come to tea.

"I just know, so there," cried Twm. Eh dear! he thought. If she comes, Gran will see right away that she is a teg. "She told me yesterday how busy she was," said Twm. "Everybody is asking her to tea."

"That will soon wear off," said Gran.

"And when it does we will ask her," said Twm's dada. "Now off to school, boyo. And pay attention, Twm. Show respect."

"Aye, Dada," said Twm scrambling through the door.

"Hey," called his father, "don't you kiss Mam any more?"

Twm rushed back to peck Mam on her plump cheek. She held him close for an instant. Dada smiled at both of them, and when he smiled, it made a warmth in Twm.

"I'll be the first one in school today," he promised, and meant it.

Grancher followed Twm to the doorstep. He closed the door and glanced up the street. "What a pity you have to go to school, lad; but perhaps if we went now, you could sing for the auditioners and still get to school on time."

"Grancher, it is most of a mile to the town hall," Twm said. "No, I'm going to be early for once, and anyway, I'm too big for the part."

"Never can tell, Twm. You be little for your age. And when they hear that voice, you are sure to win."

Twm looked at his grancher earnestly. "You really think so?"

"Aye, boy. Think of the honor singing on a real stage, and getting paid. Think what your mam could do with all that money. You know, Twm, your father is only working three days a week, and I have only my pension."

"I'll hurry home from school," Twm promised.

"Might be too late, boyo. Everyone in the valley will be competing."

"But none with a voice like mine, Grancher?"

"None with a voice like yours, Twm. You had better go on to school, boyo," said Grancher sadly.

"I'll be home early, Grancher."

Twm hurried away. Poor Grancher. Pity he had never been the great singer he dreamed of being.

"Twm, mun!"

"Gypsy, what is it, boyo?"

"I've been waiting for you for ages."

"Gypsy, what is it?"

Big tears were leaving tracks down Gypsy's grimy face. He was running, waving to Twm to follow. When they came to a dusty hawthorn tree, Gypsy was still crying. No sound he made in that sobbing. He handed Twm something wrapped up in an old jersey. It was Gypsy's weasel, dead and still.

Twm gasped. "Gypsy!" was all he could say, for Twm knew that Gypsy had treasured the weasel more than anything. "How did it happen?"

Gypsy reached for the weasel, and sat weeping and pressing the dead creature to his face. For minutes Twm stood there kicking stones. He knew that words were useless.

And Gypsy went on crying.

"Look, now," Twm said gently, "there is more than one weasel. That old thing was a rabbit-eater anyway. I will go to Sam Poacher and ask him to give you another, and we will train him proper."

"The widow did it," sobbed Gypsy at last. "She set her Welsh terrier on him, just because he took one of her old, stinking, pet rabbits. She never said a word about all the wild ones my weasel caught for her. I'd like to . . ." Gypsy banged his fist against the tree.

"Gypsy, he is dead, boyo. Crying won't bring him back."

Gypsy stared at Twm, and then he wiped his eyes and nose on his sleeve. "Twm Tybach, do you think much of me?"

"We be friends for a long time."

Gypsy gave another sob. "You be magic, Twm," he added earnestly. "Will your magic bring him back?"

Twm looked doubtfully at the weasel. "I don't think it works on weasels," he said. Then he saw Gypsy's face pucker up again. "Well now, it might. Perhaps if I rubbed the weasel in my hair." He took it from Gypsy and rubbed and rubbed, but the weasel remained stiff as a board.

"You be not magic," yelled Gypsy.

"Heisht. I know, Gypsy. Gran said the magic works best in the full moon. Hide the weasel behind a bush. Come to school now with me, and we will wait until the full moon."

"Go to the devil," said Gypsy with fire in his eyes, and taking the creature under his arm he walked away. "You be not magic," he accused, "you be not anything."

Twm watched as he turned in the opposite direction to school, bending to the hill on his way to Proud Parry's land.

"I said I would try again in moonlight," Twm called.

Not even a look back. Gypsy just left Twm standing there. Twm had lost another friend. Nothing to do but go to school. He took a shortcut, but dived behind a tree pretty sharp when he saw Mortimer and Willy climbing the hill. Twm had had enough trouble for one morning. He was determined to be at school on time, but his heart was heavy over Gypsy.

5

THE SCHOOL DAY started off so well that Twm almost forgot Gypsy. The class did sums with bundles of sticks and they used pieces of taffy for counters. They could keep the taffy if they got the sums right. Twm learned to multiply six times nine which surprised him, and he decided it was as far as he needed to go.

In composition Miss Olson let them write about anything they pleased—about the wind, a cat, a bird, the dingle. The mention of the dingle painfully reminded Twm that he had promised to take Miss Olson there. And it brought back Gypsy and the weasel. Still, there was nothing to be done about Gypsy. He was gone.

"It's such a nice day, class," Miss Olson said. "What do you say if we go outside and do history?"

"History outdoors!" whispered Mortimer with unbelieving delight.

Twm nodded happily. He was glad that Mortimer wasn't holding a grudge. For now that Gypsy was gone, Twm would need friends.

"The secret meeting is after school by the hollow tree," said Mortimer as they opened their desks.

Twm nodded wisely. "I'll be there," he said, forgetting his promise to Grancher.

Wonderful it was to get away from the classroom that reeked of boys' boots, girls' hair, blue ink and pencil shavings. They all swooped out into the fresh air.

Miss Olson told them about the time that she and her brother lived for two whole weeks in the woods of Maine. And there wasn't a murmur as she told of how they had burned out a shelter in a giant tree until it was a snug cave. They ate acorn pancakes and soup from turtles they caught, and Twm became less and less sorry he had invited her to the dingle. She was a teg and no mistake.

"Why did you go into the woods and live?" asked Gerwin.

"We ran away," she said.

A murmur went up in the class. Careful, thought Twm.

"Only Gypsies run away in our valley," said Gerwin primly.

"Then Gypsies must have fun," she said.

And then the headmaster came strolling by.

"Studying nature, is it?" he said to Miss Olson.

Twm shivered despite the sun. All the class suddenly looked

frightened, except Miss Olson. She just smiled her lovely smile and said: "We are supposed to be doing history."

"Supposed to be?" said the headmaster in a terrible voice.

"Yes, but we got to talking about running away from home instead."

"Dear, dear," said the headmaster going pink, especially his nose which looked like a piece of blotting paper.

The class huddled together now in a shy cluster, wishing they were safe in the classroom and not sitting in the middle of the field.

"Well, Miss Olson, all I can say is that this is most unusual."

The headmaster went away, as Twm said later, like a cricket in a fit. And when he did their confidence seeped back.

Why should she be afraid of old Evans anyway, Twm thought. She could turn him into a pig, or a dog, or a hare if she wanted to. Yes, she was a teg and no mistake, and Twm was so glad that she was a teg. She would teach him how to fly and goodness knows what else. She would teach him everything about magic. And then Twm would help Gypsy. Yes, he would cast a spell on the widow so that she would never be mean to Gypsy again.

Twm and the others returned to the classroom. Now the best part of the day was coming, the rehearsal of the pageant. And Miss Olson would know Twm could sing.

All the children were standing in the hall waiting to go

into the big room. Along the corridor they stood in their costumes, everyone disguised with beards, false noses, bootblacking and wigs. For this was one of the dress rehearsals. As Twm passed he saw a tiny girl dressed in a fairy costume. Her wings were all glittering, like cobwebs after the rain. How much prettier they were than anyone else's. He dared to touch one and the wing came off in his hand. The little girl started to cry.

"I might have known that you would be behind some mischief, Twm Tybach," said Miss Davies bearing down on him. "Why did you do that?"

"I didn't mean to, honest," said Twm earnestly.

"Well, you can just go into my room," she snapped. "I will deal with you later. Picking on a little girl, honestly!"

"What is the matter?" asked Miss Olson. "Twm, did you do this?"

"I didn't mean to. I just wanted to feel the wing."

"Gerwin can take his part," said Miss Davies. "Run along to my room, Twm."

"But he didn't mean to," said Miss Olson. "It was an accident."

"Twm, go to my room," said Miss Davies, but Twm stood looking pleadingly at Miss Olson.

"Twm!" thundered Miss Davies.

"Run along to her room, Twm," said Miss Olson.

And as Twm trudged along he could hear Miss Olson's voice rise . . . "But Miss Davies, he loves all flying things."

"I think I know what this boy is like," said Miss Davies frostily. "Yes, I know him well . . . I know him well." She saw him looking back and pointed to her office. "Now go and wait for me in there. Did you hear me? Did you hear me?" Twm scrambled away to Miss Davies's office.

There, he waited and waited. He heard Gerwin's voice singing his part and Twm wanted to die. What would Grancher say if he lost the part? What would Mam and Dada say? All because he accidentally broke that wing. He paced up and down the small room. The sticky sunshine came from the window lying in bars of light on Miss Davies's desk. Aye, just like jail, he thought, and for one wild moment he wanted to climb out the window and run away with Gypsy.

After what seemed like hours, Miss Davies came in. She told Twm that it was going to be decided by a board of teachers if Twm would have the part of king of the tegs. He had been warned, and still he had been tardy twice.

"But my mam has already made the costume," Twm cried.

"Well, you should have thought of that," snapped Miss Davies. "As far as I am concerned you do not deserve the part. Gerwin is reliable and sings very well, very well. You have wasted the whole afternoon with your mischief . . . the whole afternoon . . . see, there goes the bell, there goes the bell."

"I'm out of the pageant then, miss?" Twm said tearfully.

"I have told you that it is up to the board." She looked at

Twm sadly. "Why won't you learn that school is not a play yard, Twm. Not a play yard. Now you had better go. Perhaps this will teach you. Perhaps it will."

Twm walked home sadly. He knew what he must do. He must get the part in the pantomime to make up for this. If only he wasn't too late.

"Coming to the meeting?" Mortimer said.

Twm shook his head.

"You sick or something?"

"No . . . yes . . . I don't feel very well."

"That's no excuse," said Mortimer.

But Twm was too unhappy to argue. He just started running. And all down the long echoing hill he heard Mortimer's voice calling, "Teacher's babby. Teacher's babby." But worst of all was the voice inside him repeating over and over: "Gerwin Thomas has my part. Gerwin Thomas has my part." Gypsy, where was Gypsy? Twm longed suddenly with all his heart to have Gypsy back.

6

"Heisht, Twm."

Twm spun around. That voice could only belong to Gypsy
. . . "Gypsy. You?"

"What's the matter, Twm?"

"Gerwin has my part in the pageant."

"Never."

"Aye, all because of that old Miss Davies."

"Why don't you come away and hide with me?"

"I can't, Gypsy. I have got to get this part in the pantomime."

"Why?"

The question caught Twm off guard. "I don't know . . .
Grancher just expects it. And Mam and Dada will be disappointed." Twm looked at Gypsy. "I thought you were running away for good. Did you get afeared, Gypsy?"

"Never," cried Gypsy hotly. "I just decided to give your magic another chance. In the full moon, you said, it would work."

"Aye, Gypsy. You never can be sure, mind. It depends on many things."

"What things?"

"Hey, Gypsy, aren't you afraid to stand around here talking like this? The kit-catcher will surely be out looking for you because you mitched school again."

"The widow had to go to St. Teilo's market to buy some ducks today," said Gypsy.

"What difference does that make to the kit-catcher?"

"Well, the widow isn't there, see, and so the catcher will get tired of waiting. After all he does have other houses to go to. I'm not the only one to mitch school. Say, Twm, the other teachers don't like that American teacher, do they?"

"How do you know?"

"I sneaked back into school looking for you, mun, and I heard old Miss Davies and the headmaster going on about her. They were saying something about her ruining everything."

A ball of fear grew in Twm's stomach. "What else did they say?"

"I can't remember exactly. Something about her undoing things, and about watching her closely."

"Gosh, it looks bad for her."

"And worse for me," interrupted Gypsy. "Isn't that the catcher talking to the widow on the shop step? She came back early."

"Aye, mun," said Twm fearfully. "What will . . . ?"

Gypsy had already fled in the opposite direction. Fortunately the widow and the catcher had their backs to Twm. He continued on walking innocently past them. He overheard the catcher say:

"Well, if you keep threatening him with the workhouse and reform school, of course the boy will keep running away."

"What else can I do to keep him from trouble?" She saw Twm. "Make him tell you where Gypsy is," she screeched. "He knows, he knows. Two of a kind."

In one hand the widow carried an enormous green umbrella, and in the other a wicker basket, from which protruded the heads of three frightened ducks. The widow's face was rather like a duck's, with a nose that was pointed as a beak which she directed at Twm.

"Do you know where Gypsy is?" asked the catcher sternly.

"No indeed," said Twm, which was true. Gypsy could be anywhere by now. Perhaps he was hiding in a tree, or a cave. He could be in Proud Parry's blacksmith shop, or swinging high in the air on a coal ram. Twm wished with all his heart he had gone with him.

"He does know," said the widow hooking his arm with her umbrella. "Just look at that guilty face, look you."

Twm wriggled like a moth on a pin, but the widow had a strong arm.

"Make him tell," she insisted. "Heisht," said the catcher.

Quack, quack, quack went the frightened ducks, and they twisted their little heads as if pleading with Twin to save them.

"Now try and remember where you saw him last, Twm."

"I don't remember," cried Twm.

"Don't believe him," screeched the widow.

Quack, quack, quack went the ducks.

"Treated that Gypsy like one of my own," said the widow, "and what thanks do I get? His dirty old weasel got three of my best breeding rabbits."

"Let the boy go, ma'am," said the catcher.

"Not until he tells what he knows. Now where is Gypsy?"

"I don't know, I don't know," sobbed Twm, who was so happy to see his grancher scurrying down the street that he could have died with relief.

"Grancher, Grancher!" he wailed.

Grancher came as fast as his crooked legs would carry him. He looked at the catcher, bowed to the widow, and said: "Good day to you, Widow . . . Catcher." Then he turned to Twm: "What is all this about, Twm, bach? We will be too late for the contest, mun, unless we hurry."

The widow had let go of Twm by now, and turned pleadingly to Grancher and said: "Make Twm tell us where Gypsy be. He's gone again."

"Twm," said Grancher, "do you know where he be?"

"I don't know, Grancher . . . I don't know, but they won't believe me."

"Well, I believe you, boyo," replied Grancher.

"He does know where he is," cried the widow.

"Madam," said Grancher, "if you cannot control your charge, I think you should consult Parry. I didn't think it was ever a good idea giving Gypsy to your care. You spoil him one minute, and punish him the next. But that is no reason why you should go around saying that my grandson tells lies."

"You tell lies yourself," screeched the widow, "all those lies about what a great singer you were. You never went any farther than the valley pump."

"That is so unkind, Widow, and so foolish I won't even bother to argue. Good day to you, good day, Catcher. Come, Twm."

The widow's voice followed them up the street. It wasn't until they were halfway up the hill that Twm remembered he was hungry.

"Grancher," he complained, "I had no tea. I can't sing on an empty stomach."

"I've got the very things, Twm," said Grancher. "Bull's-eyes."

Twm took the bag of sweets eagerly. He loved bull's-eyes,

and they tasted wonderful once he had sucked the tobacco flavor from them. He did wish that Grancher would not keep them in the same pocket as the thick tobacco twist. Sucking and panting, Twm followed Grancher up the hill.

"Let's stop for a whiff," said Grancher, who was panting. "You will have no breath for singing, boyo. I hope you are doing your breathing exercises. You will need all your chest muscles to be king of the tegs. How is the pageant coming, anyway?"

Twm wished with all his heart that Grancher hadn't brought that up.

"They would never let me be king of the tegs," Grancher continued. "My hair was always black as night."

"You could have worn a wig."

"Aye, but it wouldn't be the same."

"Grancher, did you know that Gypsy lost his weasel?"

"No, I didn't. How did you know, Twm? I thought you hadn't seen him."

"I saw him on the way to school," said Twm crossing his fingers. "He was running away because the widow's terrier killed the weasel. Grancher, did you ever hear of a weasel being brought back to life?"

"No, Twm."

"Do you suppose Gran has?"

"Aye, she's sure to. We had better go now, boyo."

"You ever see any magic, Grancher?"

"Yes, indeed. I see and hear it every time I hear and see a great singer."

"No, no, Grancher, I mean the kind of magic that brings a dead weasel back to life again."

"Twm," said Grancher, "death is part of life. No one should want to return. I bet that weasel is in a much better heaven than he found here on earth, but there's sorry I be for Gypsy, mind, Twm."

"He was just an old rabbit-eater anyway," said Twm, "but Gypsy keeps harping and harping about . . . Grancher, see all those people coming out of the town hall? We are too late."

"Eh dear," said Grancher sadly, and Twm wished with all his heart that he hadn't been late and kept after school.

"Too late, too late," shouted Mrs. Thomas, who was coming out of the hall like a ship in full sail. "Our Gerwin is one of the finalists. I'm just going home to get his father to come and see him win."

"Better go home, Grancher."

But Grancher pushed Twm past the droves of people who were scurrying out.

"Too late, too late," called a white-haired judge.

"We just wanted to stay and listen," replied Grancher.

"You wouldn't if you had been listening all day," said the judge. Twm watched the five judges who were busy scribbling on paper, and the five smirking boys who had been chosen as finalists. Gerwin Thomas was among them, of course. He must not get this part too, Twm thought.

"Grancher," he whispered, pointing to Gerwin, "I can sing rings around him."

"Mr. Tybach," said a young man coming forward, "I remember the time you won the Singing Hill Cup."

"Dai Lewis," said Grancher beaming, "and I remember you taking three firsts in the St. Teilo's finals in . . . when was that now?"

"Long time ago, Mr. Tybach."

"You had a fine voice, Dai."

"But not fine enough, Mr. Tybach. I now direct pantomimes. Who is this?" he asked pointing to Twm.

"My grandson. We were too late," said Grancher sadly.

"Pity," said Dai Lewis. "Does he sing like you?"

"He will sing better some day," replied Grancher.

"Indeed. I would like to hear him after the others have finished."

Gerwin Thomas was on the stage now, and he was singing fair. Twm had to admit that, but Twm knew he could do better.

"When all the finalists are over," said Mr. Lewis, "I want to hear this boy."

"One more won't make any difference," said one judge wearily.

"Very kind of you, I'm sure," said Grancher warmly.

By now Twm was getting really anxious. The last finalist was on the stage. The first notes of accompaniment sounded, and then the boy's voice soared into song. Twm gasped, Grancher gasped, and whispered, "What a voice . . . what power." He looked at Twm sadly. "Can't compete with him, boyo, not yet. But wait and see, your voice will get stronger."

"Ready, Mr. Tybach?" asked Dai Lewis.

"No harm in trying, Twm," said Grancher, "since we came this far." He gently shoved Twm on the stage. They asked Twm what he was going to sing, and Twm asked for Grancher's favorite . . . might as well sing "The Gray Cuckoo." Twm let his voice rip. He pitched it high to the rafters, and no question about it, Grancher was pleased. When the song came to a close, even the tired judges were smiling and nodding.

"What an honor, what an honor, Twm," Grancher was saying. "You have a part in the pantomime if your mother and father agree."

"Grancher!" Twm cried. "You mean I was better than the other boy?"

"Well, no, Twm. That boy has a part, too. Now we had better get home and tell the good news. Thank you, Dai Lewis," added Grancher warmly.

"But what part do I have, Grancher?" Twm wanted to know.

"Well, Twm," Mr. Lewis began, but Grancher interrupted. "Excuse me, Dai, but I would like to tell him."

"Aye, of course," said Dai Lewis.

"But Grancher?"

"Come, boyo, we don't want to keep these tired judges all day." He took Twm's small hand in his big one. "You will be hearing from us," he said to Mr. Lewis.

"Grancher," Twm breathed again as soon as they got outside. "Tell me, mun, about my part in the pantomime. Wait until Mortimer and Gypsy hear about this. And old Miss Davies, too."

"Aye, it is quite an honor," said Grancher, and he started to hum. Twm grew quiet. Grancher always did that when he didn't want to answer questions. He waited.

"Twm, boyo," Grancher said. "Have you any idea how lucky you are?"

"Aye, I suppose so," said Twm.

"Picked out of hundreds, boyo."

"Why, Grancher?"

"Because you have blond hair, boyo, and a sweet high voice."

"Grancher," said Twm excitedly. "Are they going to have tegs in *Babes in the Woods?*"

"No, Twm. Twm, I expect you know that in order to get ahead in the theater a singer must be prepared to play many different parts. Did you know that your grancher once played the part of a woman in the opera *Carmen?*"

"Never," laughed Twm.

"Aye, I was. In order to get to the top of the ladder I would have done anything."

"Why didn't you, Grancher? You won a lot of cups."

"That's a long unfortunate story, Twm. But no matter. You will be up there instead."

"But not playing a woman's part," Twm grinned. Then he stopped. "What part am I playing?"

"You are playing a girl's part, Twm," said Grancher. "Just like I did, see."

"What!"

"Aye, because of your blond hair and sweet voice, you . . ."

"I won't. I won't," cried Twm. "I hate girls."

"Twm."

"I won't and you can't make me." Twm was off down the hill.

"Twm," called Grancher. "This is your big chance, mun. Wait." But Twm kept going. "Twm," thundered Grancher, "wait."

Twm waited.

"Twm boy," said Grancher. "Singing in chapel and the pageant is all very well. Nothing wrong with it for a beginning. But Twm, just imagine the stage. Can't you see that big orchestra, hear the blare of the trumpets, the thunder of the drums? Think of it. A big theater, soft with carpets and golden with a thousand lights. Then they will dim on thousands and thousands of people in the opera house. And I can see you, Twm, standing there in that big spotlight . . ."

"Dressed like a girl," sobbed Twm. And suddenly he was running down the hill as though all the witches in Wales were at his heels. It had been a terrible, terrible day. He had lost his part in the pageant to Gerwin Thomas, and now Grancher wanted him to be a girl. If he ran fast enough, perhaps the sissy, girl-like tears would dry up. Twm didn't mind being small. He didn't mind having a high voice, if it really was the voice of a teg. He didn't mind any more that some of the children were afraid to sit near him. But Twm did mind very much playing the part of a girl.

7

Twм had no idea what woke him up. One minute he was dreaming, and the next he was lying awake listening to the birds squeaking like mice in the apple tree. The sky was beginning to turn blue and a morning breeze was whispering at the window.

Then he remembered his dream. He was dressed in one of Morfydd's frocks, standing alone in a theater filled with boys who looked like Mortimer and Gerwin, all laughing so loudly Twm couldn't hear himself sing.

With a start, Twm remembered yesterday. Gypsy's weasel, Miss Davies telling him he would lose his part most likely, and worst of all was Grancher wanting him to be a girl in a pantomime. And then the fuss with his mother and his grandmother, both of them saying that they thought it would be wonderful for Twm to sing and be a girl in the pantomime—

and Morfydd laughing when she thought they were not look-ing. Will Dada think I should be in the pantomime? Never! Never! Still, they could certainly use the money now that Whitsuntide was coming. Twm would do anything to get money for his family. Anything but singing in a girl's frock. No, his father wouldn't make him do that.

Twm's mind went over some of the magic his gran talked about. She had said that if you made a cross mark with a wet finger on the head of a toad in the full of the moon, three wishes would come true.

Twm knew that there was a toad in the garden. He had seen him many times. There wasn't a moon but it was worth a try. It was better than lying in bed worrying.

He crept out of bed and tiptoed downstairs. The smell of last night's supper greeted him in the kitchen. He dressed fast, for the spring mornings were still cold. Then he crept towards the kitchen door. The lock squeaked and snapped, but Twm got outside and clicked the door shut behind him.

It was even colder out here. He shivered. The birds were still squeaking. I bet they are warm in their nests, he thought enviously. Now, where is that toad?

Twm didn't have long to wait. He found the toad, or rather the toad found Twm. It hopped across his foot. That's double luck, thought Twm delightedly. Quickly, with one hand, he caught it. How fast its heart beat. "I won't hurt you. I won't hurt you," Twm said to the toad. Then he wet his finger and

made a cross mark on its head and the toad hopped away without a backward look.

Then Twm made his wishes . . . "I wish, I wish, I wish that Gypsy will get another weasel and stop harping about the dead one if nothing can be done for it and that he will come home. I wish, I wish, I wish I never, never have to be a girl . . . ever, ever, ever." He had one more wish . . . "I wish, I wish, I wish, more than any other of the wishes, to be able to fly." Twm felt happy after that and went back into the kitchen. He would make a nice fire and surprise Gran. He bustled around finding some dry sticks and pieces of shiny coal and lit the fire just as Gran had taught him. He was poking it into a cheerful blaze when Gran came downstairs.

"Lovely fire, Twm," said Gran in a good humor because of the warmth. "I will boil you an egg."

"Wonderful," Twm breathed as Gran popped a big pink-brown egg into the pan.

"Glad to see that you are in a better mood," said Gran. "I hope you have been giving the pantomime some thought. Wonderful opportunity, Twm."

Oh, why did she have to spoil the morning, Twm thought. He took the big black kettle out to the pump to fill. Perhaps if he made himself useful, the magic would start working faster.

"Twm," said Gran. "What time did you get up, boy?"

"Early," said Twm cautiously.

"You didn't hear anything, did you?"

"Like what?"

"Voices," said Gran. "I heard voices chanting under my window."

"Was it dark?"

"I don't remember. Aye, it must have been . . . ghostly voices chanting under the moon."

"No," said Twm. "I didn't hear them." Or did he? Was that what woke him up? "Perhaps I did hear them, Gran."

"What rubbish is this?" asked Mam coming down the stairs just as the kettle had begun to laugh and cry on the stove. "You shouldn't fill his head so," she said.

All the time that his mother was making the bread, Twm wandered restlessly about the kitchen. He was glad when his egg was ready to eat, for he wanted to get out of the kitchen quickly before his mother went on about the pantomime.

He was old enough to realize how much the money would help, but if only they would be patient, he would get all the money they would ever need by just being a teg.

"I wonder when Hywel will be home?" his mother asked. "I bet he is working double shift. Goodness knows we could use extra money with Whitsuntide coming up. More toast, Twm?" she asked.

"No, thank you," he answered, watching her face in the morning light. Twm saw how tired she looked. How he wished he might give her the things that would make her life

≫ 68 ≪

easier. But please, he asked, don't let's talk about panto-mime.

"You must be sick," she said. "Aye, you do look pale, Twm. Let me see your tongue."

Twm ran out his tongue for her inspection. "It's not coated, but you do look peaked," she sighed. "I hope you are not coming down with something."

"I'm all right, Mam, honest," Twm said. "Can I do anything for you before I go to school . . . carry coal or water?"

"Sure you are feeling all right?"

"Aye, mun," Twm replied.

"Here is your lunch," said Gran. "I was just telling Twm that I hoped he had thought about the panto——"

But Twm fled through the door and by the time he stopped running, he was on top of Warm Turn Hill. "The magic certainly takes time," he muttered. He was just turning the corner when he saw Gypsy. His face was scrubbed and he was carrying school books. The magic was working at last, although Gypsy didn't look very happy.

"They caught you?" Twm asked.

"No," said Gypsy. "I went back. I got a good going over from the widow on account of my clothes," he said. "And she said next time for sure I will go to the workhouse. I would have gone this time but the catcher put in a good word for me because I came back myself."

"What made you come back by yourself, Gypsy?"

"I had to see if your magic works. Aye, and I'm sorry I came back. The widow is for everlasting telling how ashamed she is of me. You know what she did?"

"No."

"She fetched the preacher and he took me into the front room and told me to pray. He said I should pray for forgiveness and I say, why don't the widow pray for forgiveness, she killed my weasel. But he kept harping and harping. So I prayed for the Lord to forgive me and the widow—the widow mostly, though, 'cause she killed the weasel. And what did I get for my trouble? A going over from the widow after the preacher left. That's what you get for your prayers."

"You think magic works better?"

"Aye, mun. And it will work during the full moon, Twm. I buried the weasel in a safe place. I bet that old weasel will be surprised when he finds himself chasing down rabbit holes again. You can do it in the light of the moon, can't you, Twm?"

"There you go, Gypsy, harping, harping," said Twm sourly.

"But you said you could," said Gypsy passionately. Twm felt a twinge of worry. Some of the magic was working all right. It had brought Gypsy back. The toad was sure to keep off more bad luck, but still it wasn't in the light of the full moon so he could not expect to hold off all bad luck. There was still the girl part in the pantomime hanging over him, and losing his part in the pageant.

Once in school it was soon evident to Twm that something was working. He got three points higher than Gerwin for his composition and only five words wrong in dictation. And when Miss Olson whispered to him that she knew he could do it, Twm was convinced that the teg was using her magic, too.

Twm felt it was about time, mind, that he had good luck or magic working for him. He had had enough bad luck and worry the past few days to last him forever.

8

AFTER SCHOOL Twm beat the others to the dingle. There were things he wanted to do by himself.

He wanted to visit the otter who played along the banks of the Tywie River, and the curlew birds. He wanted to hear larks singing in the clear blue sky and the splash of brooks down the mountainside.

Up and up the mountain he went, hands in pockets, whistling away fit to lose his front teeth, as Gran would say. Over Proud Parry's gate, stepping over the newborn lambs, Twm wondered how many days old they were. Then he stood and gasped. Stretching as far as he could see were blue-bells, just as though a piece of the sky had fallen out. He plucked the juicy root of a bluebell. It left the brown earth with a sucking sound. Sweet it was to the taste.

He walked softly now past the old forge where Proud

Parry's blacksmith changed the horses' shoes. Trouble Twm would have if the blacksmith found him. Enemies to the right and the left when you are young, Twm thought. He ran along the canal banks, made faces at the old black bull. The bull charged, but Twm got out with time to spare.

"I'd rather be chased by you, black bull, than by Proud Parry's blacksmith or his gamekeeper," Twm whispered as he ran over the little wooden bridge past the board that said "No Fishing or Hunting!" Panting now, he lay down on a bank of moss.

What was this? Over there, a bit to the left, Twm saw two eyes watching. Motionless stood a badger, wakeful. The creature hoped to be missed in the dingle stillness. Twm sauntered toward him whistling, pretending to be not the least bit interested in badgers. Then, just as the badger made for his hole, Twm leaped. Though the badger kicked with his feet, sending up a shower of dirt to blind him, Twm held on to his back legs, gripping his tail. The earth rumbled to the thunder of the badger's rage. The badger's bellowing and roaring was for all the world like Gran's when he forgot to close the chicken pen. Twm let go and walked away, laughing.

The river flashed in the sunlight, and the thrush cried, *Don't you hear me? Don't you hear me?*

"I do, I do," answered Twm, and up the tree he went fast as a squirrel. A nest of baby thrushes welcomed him with open mouths.

"When did you hatch?" he asked delightedly, taking one of the bare birds in his hand while the old mother was flying around complaining worse than Twm's mother on washday. Twm came back down the tree and waited, wishing that Gypsy Joe would hurry, and the rest of the gang, too. Twm had seen his creatures now and wanted to have fun.

"What was that?" Twm heard a shuffling in the bush. Grancher Badger again, or was it a flap of wings? Gamekeeper, perhaps? Twm listened, his heart pounding in his breast. It sounded too light for the gamekeeper. He gripped his hands in his pockets, swallowing dry in his mouth.

"Who's there?" he asked when he couldn't stand it any longer.

"It's me, Twm," answered a soft voice.

"Indeed to goodness," Twm said disgustedly. It was Benja Bowen, a grade lower in school, and not a day over seven. Benja stood there scrawny as a bantam rooster scratching his left leg with his right-shoe toe.

"Why aren't you in school?" accused Twm.

"I've been sick with measles," replied Benja. "My mam sent me out for fresh air."

"You'd better go home," Twm said. "You don't want the gamekeeper to catch you."

"I bet you are mitching," said Benja admiringly.

"I am not," Twm answered indignantly. "Go on, go home."

"Want a bite of my taffy apple?" asked Benja.

Twm's mouth watered. "I don't mind," he answered.

"You can have one little bite, or three good licks," replied Benja.

"Righto," said Twm obligingly, grabbing it in his hand. He sniffed the delicious smell of Welsh taffy covering the juicy apple.

"You took a lick and a bite," yelled Benja, "a big bite."

"No, indeed," said Twm, "it came off in my mouth."

"You like taffy apples?" asked Benja slyly. "You really like 'em?"

"Aye," replied Twm, who was hungry enough to eat a dozen.

"If I give you this one . . . all of it," said Benja, "will you do something for me?"

Twm eyed the apple, and his stomach rumbled. "Aye," he answered reaching for it.

"Anything, mind," said Benja.

"Aye."

"Then you get me into the secret society," he said as Twm polished off the apple.

"I can't do that," protested Twm. "The others have to vote on you, and you had better go now. They do awful things to people who hang around."

"What do they do?"

"Hang you by your toes from a tree," replied Twm.

"You had better go. I think I can hear the boys coming."

"I'm staying," said Benja. "You took my apple, and I'm staying. I have two other apples in my pocket." And Benja took out the other apples and held them under Twm's nose.

"How in the world did you get three?" asked Twm.

"My mam was making them for the chapel bazaar, and when she wasn't looking . . ."

Twm wasn't listening. He could hear Mortimer and Gypsy now, hooting like owls in the distance. He wished they would hurry.

Mortimer and Gypsy came panting up the hill red-faced. Mortimer's eyes on fire. Behind them came Willy, Gerwin and Jethro.

"Why didn't you wait for us?" Mortimer demanded. But then he saw Benja. "What is he doing here?"

Twm looked at Benja like he had only just noticed him. "I don't know."

"Let's start the meeting," said Willy, "or the day will be gone."

"Aye," replied Mortimer, "but what is this babby doing here?"

"You brought him, Twm," Mortimer cried.

"I did not," Twm answered.

"Aye," said Willy, "you'll be inviting girls next, Twm."

"Never," Twm said passionately.

"Shoo, shoo," yelled Mortimer.

"Twm said I could stay," replied Benja in a quivering voice.

"I did not," said Twm hotly. "He's been following me around."

"Shoo, shoo," yelled Mortimer again.

"Want a lick of my apple?" asked Benja, sticking it under Mortimer's nose. "See, I have two."

"I don't mind," answered Mortimer.

"Same, same for me," said Willy as he and the other boys crowded around Benja.

"I'll be seven and three-quarters next month," said Benja, watching them lick and nibble.

"That's a lie," stated Gerwin.

"I can show you my birth card."

"If he stays, I don't," said Mortimer wiping his lips after finishing the apple.

Benja started to howl, "You took my apple, you took my apple."

"Let him stay," said Gypsy.

"Aye, let him stay," said Twm.

"I resign," shouted Mortimer.

"Same. Same," said Gerwin.

Benja dug into his pockets and produced some gumdrops. "If I give you these, can I stay?"

"I resign," shouted Willy. "If he stays, I resign."

But Benja and the gumdrops stayed, and none resigned.

"Get in a circle," called Mortimer. "We have wasted enough time." He opened his coat and pulled out two large darning needles from the lapels of his jacket. "Now don't lose these. I had an awful job getting them out of my mother's sewing box."

Each boy sat in the circle and pricked the ball of his thumb on the left hand. In time, after they squeezed, each got enough blood to press his thumb on a piece of birch bark. Then they chanted in Welsh that they would suffer slow fire rather than keep any secrets from the society, and suffer slow death rather than tell any secrets of the society.

Twm managed to keep his right hand in his pocket during the oath. He crossed his fingers. Later he would cross his eyes and kiss his elbow for he just couldn't tell them about Miss Olson coming to the dingle.

"Death will come to those who blab," they chanted. Meeting had begun.

9

"RIGHT THEN," said Mortimer. "What shall we do to prove that this is the best secret society in the world?"

Twm pondered. "Blacksmith Gwallter," he said finally. "But it doesn't count 'less we see the fire in his eyes."

"Never," said Gerwin going pale.

Twm looked at Gerwin sourly. Not worth his salt, he decided. Thin as a whip, and sissy as a girl. Why did Mortimer bother with him? Always sniffing with a dewdrop on his nose. He and Willy should be called "Ditto." They were both sissy, and echoed everything Mortimer said.

"Well?" said Twm impatiently.

"Well?" said Mortimer.

"Blacksmith Gwallter it is," Twm insisted.

"Righto," cried Gypsy, his dark eyes dancing.

"What if he catches us?" asked Gerwin.

"I don't know," admitted Mortimer. "He never caught me."

"Brand you with an iron," said Gypsy wickedly.

"No! How do you know that?" Twm wanted to know.

"That's what the widow said."

"Can't be true, can it?" asked Mortimer with concern, and Gerwin started shivering like a custard.

"Aye," said Gypsy. "True as the Bible. The widow doesn't lie."

"Perhaps we better do something else to prove ourselves," suggested Mortimer.

"You afeared?" asked Gypsy.

" 'Course not. Only the others, the little ones, like Benja, is what I be thinking of."

"I'm not afeared," said Benja.

"Well I'm not going to do it," stated Gerwin. "My mam wouldn't like it."

"Same, same exactly," said Willy.

"Not worth it," added Jethro.

"Are we a good gang or not?" asked Gypsy.

"As a matter of fact, I remember now my mam saying I had to go right home after school," said Gerwin turning away.

"Babby!" shouted Mortimer.

"I am not."

"You are, too."

"But . . ."

"No buts," cut in Mortimer. "Go, if you be afeard."

"I'll stay," said Gerwin.

"Right then," replied Mortimer. "Follow me."

The seven boys crept toward the blacksmith's forge. Seven pairs of eyes peered through the window at the smith. His big black head was sunk on his chest, and his legs were thrust out before the fire. Another peep, and a listen to his snores, and they tiptoed closer.

"Who's first?" whispered Twm. "You, Gypsy?"

Gypsy nodded excitedly. "I'll get a lock of his hair," he whispered taking out his penknife, and away he went swift and silent as a deer. He was back in a minute. Twm looked at him with blind, helpless admiration. "Gosh! Gypsy!"

Mortimer looked at the hair, and then at Gypsy with distrust. "All this jawing," he said, "about a lock of hair."

"Better write that down," said Twm. "Gypsy proved himself brave."

"Write that down," replied Mortimer sourly, "though it doesn't really count, 'cause he didn't see the fire in his eyes."

"It does so," said Twm.

"It still doesn't count, I said," Mortimer yelled.

"Heisht!" said Twm. "Do you want to wake up the smith?"

Another peep through the window and a listen. The smith was still snoring.

"I say it still doesn't count," said Mortimer. "Gypsy didn't see the fire in his eyes."

"He got the hair," said Twm. "It stands to reason that getting Gwallter's hair is worse than seeing fire in his eyes. If you don't think so, you try it, Mortimer."

"If we all take a lock, he'll be bald," said Jethro.

"Your turn, Gerwin," said Mortimer.

"Why my turn? Twm wants to go next. Don't you, Twm?"

"Your turn, Gerwin," said Twm.

"I'll go," said Benja.

"Later," said Twm. "Now come on, Gerwin," he ordered, "or out of the society."

He gave him a shove and Gerwin stumbled through the door. The smith awoke with a start. And when he saw Gerwin and Twm right behind he didn't wait to ask questions. He flung himself out of the chair and made a grab for them, but the boys were already out and away. When the gang stopped running, they were practically down the mountain.

"What will we do now?" Mortimer asked between panting breaths.

"I'm going home," Gerwin said.

"Aw, come on, Gerwin," said Twm. "That was fun and

you saw the fire in the smith's eyes. Come to think about it, so did I. Now it's your turn, Mortimer.''

"Twm," said Benja, "I'll go next if you will come with me.''

"It won't count if I do," said Twm cautiously.

"Yes it will," said Mortimer. "You brought Benja. He's younger than the rest of us. You show him.''

"You're the leader," said Twm.

"I'll show him if you're afeared," said Gypsy.

"I'll show him," said Twm. "Come on, Benja.''

Back to the forge again Benja and Twm crept. In through the door they went, Twm first before he lost his courage. Benja was right behind him.

Blacksmith Gwallter rubbed his eyes unbelievingly. He lunged towards the lads and this time he didn't miss. He caught Twm and Benja in a grip of iron. Twm called for help, but the rest of the gang disappeared like a shoal of minnows.

"What do you two think you are doing?" roared the smith. And without waiting for an answer, he cracked their heads together like a couple of nuts. "I have work to do enough without watching out for you two." And he shook them like Welsh terriers. "Now out of here with you and if I see your faces again, you will go in there." He pointed to the blazing fire. "And tell Gypsy Joe that if I see him around I will fry him

slow." He spat in the fire sending up a hiss of steam. "Out," he said, using his big boatlike boot.

The gang gathered around Twm and Benja. "What did he do?" they wanted to know.

"He said that he would burn us if we went in there again," said Benja rubbing his head.

"I wonder why he didn't burn you this time?" asked Gypsy.

"Aye," said Mortimer.

"Aye," said Willy. "What did you do to stop him?"

Twm blinked. All the gang were looking at him and Benja.

"Why didn't he, Twm?" Benja asked.

"Well," said Twm, suddenly enjoying the look of horror on the faces around him. "Well, I cast a spell over him. Yes, that's what I did. I cast a magic spell over him."

"Aye," said Benja. "That's what we did."

"I knew you could do it, Twm," said Gypsy admiringly. "I just knew you could do it. You be magic, Twm. And you'll bring back my weasel."

"Well, Gypsy, it doesn't work unless it's a 'mergency."

"The ferret is a 'mergency isn't it, Twm?" asked Gypsy. "I know you can do it, Twm."

"Aye," said Twm, throwing caution to the wind. "I suppose I can do most anything."

Mortimer was kicking stones. Suddenly he turned to Twm and shouted: "All right, all right, so you be magic. But what are we going to do now?"

"Ring doorbells?" Twm suggested.

"Break windows?" said Benja.

"That's babby's stuff," said Mortimer. "Perhaps you would like to make mudpies?"

"Chalk words in the chapel?" said Willy.

"Tie things on the lamp post?" said Jethro.

"No, no, no," thundered Mortimer. "It must be something special."

"Ride on the coal trams," said Gypsy. "That's if you are not all afeared."

"Never," said Twm. "They will send us to the reformatory for that. And we will get a blister from our dadas as well, mun."

"Only if they catch us," said Gypsy. "I do it all the time."

"But what if we get caught?" said Willy.

"We can't with Twm's magic," argued Gypsy.

"That's right. That's right," shouted Twm, still drunk with power.

"So, come on, mun," said Gypsy. "We won't get caught."

"Na, we won't get caught. Come on," shouted Twm. "Come on, gang."

Down the mountain they ran. They crossed the old iron bridge, and met a group of coal-black, tired colliers coming the other way. The gang huddled closer together.

"Where do you think you are going?" one miner asked.

"Taking the shortcut home," said Twm.

"Righto," said the miner, "but don't go near those coal trams, son."

They waited until the miners were out of sight and then the boys ran towards the steam-swept colliery grounds. They avoided wire ropes and rails and running trams. From the house-high stacks of rusty pit props came the woody smell of splintered pine. They could hear the mine's metallic sound. They passed the miners who were working on the pit top.

"Go on with you," called one, "and don't get near that mine shaft."

As soon as the miner's back was turned Twm and his friends crouched down behind an old tram that was standing still. They were inches away on an archway above the mouth of the mine itself. They stared at the dark tunnel. They watched the down-tilted rail tracks disappearing into the earth. One glittering wire rope ran swiftly down the slant over its roller out of sight into the tunnel beneath them, and its fellow passed up in the other direction.

The boys' eyes grew big as they watched the noisy tram come up the slope out of the mine. Seven cars loaded with lumps of shiny coal were being tugged up. A young collier, wearing a naked light flaming on his cap, rode hunched in the first car. He didn't see the gang. He seemed to see nothing, not even the empty tram going the other direction right beside him.

"We jump the last car," shouted Gypsy.

They waited and waited. When the final car was about to pass, the boys jumped on for a free ride up the mountain. But Benja got confused and jumped on the tram going the other way into the steam-swept mines.

Twm saw Benja first. He gasped and almost fainted, too stunned to speak. He pointed frantically to where Benja was heading, down, down, down the slope. Gypsy saw Benja disappear into the mine, waving his small hands.

"Stop," yelled Twm.

Gypsy just shook his head. "We can't stop the tram," he screamed to Twm. "We must wait till it stops and we can catch one going the other way."

Up and up they went, Twm quaking and shaking and wondering if they ever would reach the top. Frantically he tried every magic trick he knew to make Benja come back out of that mine again. Sweat began to pour out of him. He rubbed his face and noticed just too late that his hands were coal black. Mortimer and the rest were laughing and shouting, while Twm and Gypsy sat sober as Sunday until at last the tram reached the top.

They jumped off in a panic and Mortimer was whooping around. "We did it, gang. We did it. We did it, Twm," he cried giving Twm a friendly punch.

"Benja went the other way," said Twm, in a voice as hollow as a coffin.

"Never," said Mortimer going white.

"Aye."

Mortimer was the first to recover. "Now you have done it, Twm Tybach. If he is killed, it is all your fault."

"Aye, all your fault," chorused everyone but Gypsy.

"Heisht," shouted Gypsy. "Let's think a minute, mun."

"It's his fault," cried Willy. "Now we will all go to reform school, perhaps prison, perhaps hang if he dies."

"Not me," said Mortimer in terror. "Twm Tybach, not me."

"Heisht, Mortimer," shouted Gypsy. Then he turned to Twm. "Twm, this is really a 'mergency. What will we do?"

"I don't know," said Twm, soaked in misery and fear.

"Well, you are going to prison, not me," said Mortimer.

"If Twm goes, we all go," said Gypsy. "Anyway, it will be all right. Twm will use his magic in the full moon." He said anxiously, "It will be all right, won't it, Twm?"

"I think so," said Twm doubtfully.

"It better be, boyo, 'cause I ain't going to prison," said Mortimer.

"I should have gone home," said Gerwin.

"I know," said Gypsy. "Let's get on the tram going down into the mine and look for Benja."

"Not me," said Gerwin. "I'm going home."

"Same, same exactly," said Mortimer and then the others.

"Heisht," said Gypsy. "Will you wait here, then, while Twm and I go down?"

"What?" cried Twm.

"Come on, Twm, don't be afeared," said Gypsy. "We can do it."

"Aye," said Twm, braver than he felt.

"We will wait," said Mortimer as if he were granting them a great favor.

"Right then," yelled Gypsy. "Now! Come on. Now!"

Clank, clank, clank went the old tram down the long mountain. Every clank convinced Twm that the end was near. It was hurrying now and whistling. One minute he saw Gypsy, and then darkness. The tram stopped. They were inside the cavelike coal mine.

"Gypsy!" Twm screamed.

"Heisht," said Gypsy in a wobbly voice.

"We will never get out of here, Gypsy."

"Of course we will," said Gypsy. But his voice sounded hollow. Twm felt the coal dust in his throat and chest. He could smell water, stale water, and hear the sound of picks scratching overhead. Gypsy swung his torch and Twm wished he hadn't. Being in the pitch dark was bad, but the dim light only made it worse. Men, many men, lay side by side picking coal. Why didn't the roof fall in on them?

This wasn't the way he thought it would be at all. He thought it would be like inside the caves he had once seen on a trip to Chedda Gauge, in Somerset. For sixpence you saw lovely rock formations, pretty as rainbows. But down here the ground fell from under you and you went into a darkness, so dark that it made your knees shake and bend. Twm wondered how many times his dada had come down and if he ever got over the dark dark that made you feel as if you would never see light again.

Hour after hour, it seemed, they waited there. Twm's hand stole towards Gypsy.

"Right there, boyo," said Gypsy, excited.

Then the tram crawled deeper into the pitch-black tunnel. Men stripped to the trews and lying down lengthwise were picking deep into the coal seams, stopping only to move the slag that fell when the coal was loose. Twm thought suddenly about what old Miss Davies said: "Coal was the ruination of Wales, that was once green as moss." Twm knew he was a babby, but now he would never want to go into the coal mine again.

There was so little air now that he was getting sleepy. He blinked and thought he saw his dada's face in the glitter of the coal. His head ached . . . tears stung his eyes. Would he ever see light again?

"Now be ready," whispered Gypsy. "We get the next tram going back out of here. Get ready to jump . . . *now!*" Twm missed the tram whizzing by them on its way out of the mine. He was frozen with fear.

"Come on, Twm." Gypsy's voice was getting farther and farther away. Twm was crying aloud now.

"Who's in that tram?" the voice of a miner called.

Twm crouched down as another tram went by.

"Somebody in this one," yelled the miner. "Good Lord, it's a child. Come and help me with him, mun." That must be Benja, Twm decided. Please, Benja, don't be dead.

Shouts of men coming from all over now, snatching at lamps for a closer look. Terror was in Twm; sweat flooding over him. He looked again at the roof. Gaunt were the shadows of the torch. He was getting dizzy again. Fear struck again, like a fist. He must get on an outgoing tram. He would jump on the next, the one coming now.

Closer, closer, and jump . . . "Gypsy!"

Twm somehow managed to fling himself into an outgoing tram while countless echoes reverberated from the narrow mouth of the mine.

He was alive. In the open again, and could breathe. Oh, what a joy to come up in the cool air of the afternoon again, and feel the warmth of the sun.

"All right, is it, boyo?" Gypsy asked when Twm got off at the top of the mountain.

Twm was too shaken to do more than nod.

"They got Benja."

"Aye," said Mortimer, "but we don't know how he is. He might be dead, and it's all your fault."

"Wait," demanded Gypsy. "Before any of us take an-

other step, remember we are a gang sworn to each other. Let us keep quiet about this, right?"

"Right." The whole gang applauded this idea. If Benja died, it must always be a deep secret.

Twm trudged home with Gypsy in silence.

"Don't worry, Twm, your magic will work," said Gypsy before they parted.

Twm gave Gypsy a long weary glance. "I don't know," he answered and ran from Gypsy as though a thousand demons were at his heels.

10

Twm flew home, and as soon as he got inside the door he dropped into a chair. "Gran! Gran!"

"What in the world have you been up to?" asked Gran.

Twm was thankful his mother came bustling in just then, because he was so desperate about Benja that Gran might have got his secret out of him.

"I hear Gypsy came back by himself this time," Mam said. "What a blessing that boy is finally learning to treasure his home."

"I wouldn't vouch for it," replied Gran. "That boy is still Gypsy . . . all Gypsy."

"Gran!" said Twm's mam. "How can you say that about a motherless boy? Shame."

"Motherless he may be," Gran answered, "but bad. All you need to do is look at those glittering eyes, and willful feet."

"When will Dada or Grancher be home?" asked Twm, yearning suddenly for the company of men.

"Grancher is up in the town hall trying to get you a different part in the pantomime," said Gran. "Though why should he bother when you are so ungrateful for the other part? You are missing a great chance there, boyo, to say nothing of the money."

"Aye," agreed Twm's mam. "We could certainly use the money."

Twm would have taken a dozen girl's parts in a dozen pantomimes if he could be sure that Benja wasn't dead and he never, never had to go into the mine. He wondered now why he had ever fussed about anything so unimportant as a pantomime.

"When will Dada be home?" he asked.

"Any time," said his mam. "There is quiet you are, Twm. Anything wrong?"

Twm heard the front door open. Was it Grancher? Was it Dada? Please, God, let it be one of them, Twm prayed.

"Hello, everyone." It was Dada. "I hope you have plenty of hot water, Tessa," he said cheerfully.

Twm stared at his coal-black face. He hadn't heard about Benja, then. Twm didn't know whether to be glad or sorry.

"Water is all ready, Hywel," said Mam. "Out of the kitchen everyone."

Twm was already at the door. Later, perhaps, he could talk to his father.

"Twm," said Dada, "help me down with this tin tub, boyo, and the water, is it?"

"Aye, Dada."

"How is school going?"

"I got three more points in composition than Gerwin," Twm was happy to say.

"Good, good. I hope you are singing well enough for the pageant too, boyo."

Twm's knees felt like water, and his mouth was suddenly dry as a rock. With a jolt, Twm remembered he might not have a part in the pageant.

"Well, come on, boy, move yourself before my water gets cold."

"Aye, Dada."

"Anything wrong, boyo?" he asked. "There's a long face."

"Nothing, nothing wrong, Dada."

"Worrying about the girl's part in the pantomime, is it?"

"Well, no, not exactly."

"You needn't worry any more my son. No boy of Hywel Tybach is going to play a girl's part. Now we can smile again, is it?"

Twm felt the tears sting his eyes. If his father had said

this yesterday, Twm would have whooped for joy. But how could his father know that playing a girl's part was nothing compared to perhaps being the cause of Benja's death.

"All right now, is it, boyo?"

"Aye, Dada. Thank you," said Twm heavily.

"Leave me now, boy," said Mr. Tybach. "I must take my bath, see."

Twm poked into the parlor. Grancher was there. Perhaps he could talk to him. But Grancher was looking sad. Why didn't I take that part, Twm thought. I would have been rehearsing in the town hall, and out of all this trouble.

"No other parts left, boyo," Grancher said. "But next year," he added cheerfully.

How could Twm tell Grancher that by next year he might be in prison, locked up, and living on bread and water. Well, if worse came to worst, he could always run away with Gypsy, and there was still the night of the full moon, and perhaps Miss Olson would help him with her magic. Twm just hoped that Benja's name would not come up tonight.

He looked around the room wistfully. Soon he would be leaving them forever. Morfydd would still be sitting in that chair, her pink tongue sticking out as she concentrated on her homework. Would she stop and think of him when he was in prison?

He looked at Grancher's white beard, shining silky under

the gas jet, and Gran's hands flying like two dry leaves with the veins showing as she stitched.

Mam spooning out the custard—no more custard for Twm if Benja died. But Twm found that he minded leaving Dada most. Never, if he went to prison, could he gain his respect—or if he ran away either. But if Benja died, he had to go. Prison it would be and locked up like a bird in a cage.

Twm had no appetite at supper. Dada urged him to have more custard. Twm shook his head.

"Anything wrong, son?" he asked, looking at Twm steadily.

"Nothing." Twm crossed his fingers under the table.

The terrible day ended with the choirmaster calling about the song Twm's father was composing for Whitsuntide. When Twm heard the knock at the door, he was sure it was the policeman coming for him. After seeing the kindly choirmaster standing there instead, he almost cried with relief.

"Well," said Twm's dada, "this is indeed an honor. Make room for him at the table, Tessa girl, for the musical needs feeding too, mind. Perhaps you will sing and play for him while he eats a bite, girl."

Sweet was his mam's voice that night as she sang his father's song. As Twm watched her hands ripple on the Welsh harp, he thought he would die of sadness. When the song ended he felt tears on his cheek.

"Time for bed, son," said Twm's dada after the choir-master left. "Scholars need rest. Did you hear, Tessa, that our Twm got three points higher in composition than Gerwin Thomas?"

"He never said a word," replied his mam smiling. "Well, at last he is showing some sense, is it?"

Twm wandered miserably up to bed. If he didn't talk to someone about his trouble, he knew he would burst. Gran was sitting in front of her mirror combing her thin white hair.

"Your hair is as white as mine," said Twm.

"Not born that way, just turned white," Gran corrected.

"You going bald like Grancher?" he inquired, just to have something to say.

"No. When it comes out that is healthy. Leaves room for more to grow."

Suddenly Gran slipped out of her chair and sat on the bed.

"You be in trouble, I know," she said. "If you don't tell me you will be in greater trouble, mark my words."

Twm was silent and finally Gran went back to her mirror, winding her hair into a fragile bun.

Twm pondered what to do. He couldn't tell her about Benja, but he needed to talk to someone about magic, because if ever anyone needed magic, Twm did. Finally, he blurted: "Gran, I think I can be all teg. I think I've found a way. Gran, I know a teg."

Gran put on her glasses and looked at Twm over them. In a

clear and solemn voice she said: "Don't blaspheme, Twm."

"But I do know a teg," he said excitedly.

"Never."

"Honest."

"Who is she?"

"Promise you won't tell, Gran, promise?"

"Well . . ."

"Promise?"

"Promise," she said reluctantly.

"Cross your eyes, Gran, and kiss your elbow."

"I'll cross my eyes," replied Gran, crossing them beauti-
fully, "but I can't kiss my elbow, boy, 'cause my joints creak."

"Well . . . crossing your eyes will be enough, I suppose."

"Right then, tell me who it is."

"Well, this teg is going to help me to be all teg. Going to
help me fly," said Twm breathlessly, "and help me to help
people like Dada, you, Gypsy and Ben—all kinds of people."

"Who is it?" Gran insisted.

"I'm going to show her the dingle, see, and then she will
teach me how to fly."

"Who is it?"

"Miss Olson, my teacher."

Gran unwound her hair and started to wind it up again.
Deft were her motions; her fingers flew as she coiled and
pinned, working blind without a mirror, until she had a

small, shining ball of snow. "Did she tell you this?" she asked finally.

"No, well not exactly, but I know she is a teg."

"Why?"

"By the things she does. Just this morning I caught a toad see, and all kinds of magic came about after I put a cross mark on his head with a wet finger, but she made the magic double strong, 'cause after I got to school I got three points higher than Gerwin. It was her magic that made mine work double."

"Tegs are wicked, Twm."

"But she is a good teg, Gran, and I will be a good teg, too."

"Go to bed," said Gran, "and keep away from that teg, Twm, or I will tell about her."

"You promised," said Twm outraged. "You crossed your eyes."

"But I didn't kiss my elbow. Now go to sleep and stop thinking about her. We be respectable people."

Twm hit the pillow and buried his face in it. That is the last secret she gets out of me, he thought miserably before he went to sleep.

11

By MORNING the news of Benja had flown from house to house. Everyone was telling a different tale. Some said he had been down in the mines for hours. Others said a few days. The doctor had been at Benja's side all night, the tales went, and Benja had missed going to the upper palace only by a whisker.

"He still might wear the long white shirt," Gran said darkly, looking suspiciously at Twm. "Nothing human put him there for sure."

"Now Gran," said Twm's father, "let's not start that old nonsense."

"There are tegs in this valley, I tell you," she insisted.

Twm's eyes opened imploringly at her, but she kept on.

"I wouldn't trust that blond American teacher, I can tell you."

"Mother!" thundered Twm's father. "That is a terrible

thing to even think, never mind say. Blaming a poor teacher just because she is blond, and comes from America."

Twm looked at the clock. It was almost seven-thirty. If he left now, perhaps he could find out something before he went to school. One bright hope remained. Benja was still alive. Perhaps Gypsy knew something more.

"Where are you going so early?" asked Mam.

"Oh, I just want to get an early start to school," said Twm innocently.

"Good boy," said his father. "Stay out of trouble, boyo, and work hard for the teacher."

As Twm left the room he could hear Gran's voice rising. "I vow that teacher is bewitched." His father's answered: "I tell you there are no such things as tegs." Twm didn't wait to hear more, but scrambled outside to find the rest of the secret society waiting.

For the first time in their lives, they all arrived at school early. They hung outside the iron gate in a dejected huddle. Mortimer's eyes burned with sleeplessness, and Gerwin, Jethro, Willy and Gypsy were jumpy as grasshoppers.

"Perhaps Benja is all right this morning," said Jethro hopefully.

Twm shook his head sadly. "My mam said he is shocked," replied Twm. "I wonder what that is, being shocked?"

"You mean in shock," said Mortimer. "My Uncle Waldo was shell-shocked."

"But Benja didn't go near a shell," answered Twm.

"He's coal-shocked then," shouted Mortimer, "and that is bad. What shall we do?"

"We can always run away," said Gypsy, longing for an excuse.

"I'm not running away," said Mortimer, "because I'm not to blame."

"Let's you and me run away, Twm," whispered Gypsy.

Twm shook his head. "I got to stay until after the full moon, Gypsy. Then everything will be all right."

"Why wait until then?" asked Gypsy. "Why not run while we can? By then it might be too late."

"What you two whispering about?" accused Mortimer.

"We were wondering when we would hear some news of Benja," said Twm.

"Perhaps he will come today after all," said Mortimer clutching at straws. "I bet he is all right this morning. Probably just a bump on Benja's head and soon we will see him coming round the tump or the hill."

"He won't come today," said Gerwin gloomily. "My mam said the doctor was there all night."

"He might come today," said Twm. "He had all night to get better. My mam always says children get sick fast and better fast."

"I bet he's unconscious," said Jethro darkly. "And perhaps he can't talk," he added hopefully.

But no one said what they were all thinking. Perhaps he's dead!

They waited and waited. Presently other children hove into sight. Everytime they saw a small boy coming their faces brightened. They gazed hopefully for a moment and then turned sadly away to gaze hopefully at another face.

"We better run away," urged Gypsy. "Or it's prison for us. Come on while the going is good."

"No news is good news, my grancher says," said Twm.

"We better run, Twm," said Gypsy again, "or it's prison. Bread and water."

"Not for me," said Mortimer passionately. "Come on, gang. If Gypsy wants to stay with Twm Tybach, that's his worry."

But they all stayed until at last the school bell tolled and they walked into class as though they were following a hearse.

Twm tried to fasten his mind on school, but the more he tried to listen to what Miss Olson said the more his mind wandered. Was Benja conscious now? Had he told on the gang? Was Benja's mother telling everyone in the street? Would Dada be waiting at home with the strap?

Everytime the classroom door opened, Twm's heart stopped. When the headmaster came in and looked stern as he always did, Twm half rose in his seat. He thought the end had come. But the headmaster went out.

Twm slumped back down, giving himself over to the horror. He pictured Benja's white face, his little feet stretched out before him. His mother was crying basinsful over him. But Benja didn't hear, for he was white and cold.

The policeman would be waiting for Twm. His mother would be packing his clothes in the old tin box and she would throw herself on Twm and murmur: "Why? Why? Why?"

"Continue reading, Twm Tybach." Miss Olson's voice broke into his thoughts, bringing him back from sorrow. A girl with a pink sticky face pointed to the place as Twm fumbled and mumbled.

"Twm Tybach," said Miss Olson. "What was the last paragraph about?"

Twm shook his head mournfully. "I don't know, miss."

"You have not been listening," she accused. "You haven't, have you?"

Twm shook his head again. It wasn't fair that he should be standing here when poor Benja might be dead. Everyone was acting as though they had never heard of Benja. He felt the tears sting his eyes.

"Don't you feel well, Twm?" she asked gently.

"No, miss," said Twm. And that was a fact. He knew he was white as goat's cheese.

Miss Olson came over and held his head. "Sit down, Twm," she said kindly. "Perhaps you'll be better soon."

I wonder if she knows what's happened, wondered Twm. And for one desperate moment he was about to blurt out in front of the whole class what had happened. But he remembered the gang was watching him and he sat down and swallowed hard.

He felt better at lunchtime, for Miss Olson made him stay in class while she warmed some cocoa. She also gave him a piece of chocolate cake that was better even than his mother's.

Better make the best of this, Twm thought. Tomorrow I might be on bread and water. If only Benja was all right. If Benja was well enough, everything would be fine. If he were only out in the yard right now, thought Twm, I would give him this chocolate cake. I would slip it into my pocket for Benja. Perhaps if he went outside right now, he might catch another toad. It might work. Oh, if Miss Olson would use her magic. He needed her magic now. If not, he would surely go to prison. The picture of bread and water brought such agony of suffering over him that it felt like a bad tooth. He worked it over and over again until it felt like a mouthful of aching teeth.

"You think it will be a fine day tomorrow?" inquired Miss Olson. "You still want to go to the dingle?" she asked. "That's if you feel up to it."

Twm's face suddenly beamed. "That's right," he added. "Tomorrow is Saturday. I'll meet you at the dingle."

"Well, you seemed to get well in a hurry," said Miss Olson.

"Oh yes, miss," breathed Twm. "I feel wonderful now. Tomorrow we will go to the dingle."

12

THE NEXT DAY Twm scurried out of the house and off towards the dingle before anyone was up. He swooped out into the early morning sunshine and hailed the birds. He was going off to meet the teg.

How he had tried yesterday to be good as gold. When he arrived home after school he fetched and carried coal and water, and fed the chickens. During supper he heeded Grancher's advice and let the ladies have the first skim off the rice pudding even though the water dribbled down Twm's chin and Grancher's whiskers as they watched the golden crusty top disappear. Then Twm pleased Dada by offering to go to the Band of Hope meeting with Gran, Mam and Morfydd.

"I don't know what you are up to, boyo," Gran said as she put on her shawl, "but I vouch it is no good whatever."

Twm endured the minister's droning through the sermon

of fire and brimstone without twitching too much. Gran's head soon began to nod like a top-heavy flower until the minister moved the sermon to Benja, "a lamb among wolves." That night Twm went to bed unhappy and remorseful.

Now on his way to the dingle he forgot his fear and troubles, not because they were any lighter, but because of the teg.

Soon everything would be all right. With his magic Twm could do anything, fly anywhere. The teg wouldn't let him down. By tonight he would be able to fly anywhere, unafraid of everything but hawks. Gran had said that hawks were the teg's mortal enemy, especially hawks sitting on the north side of a tree where moss grew.

By the time Twm had climbed three hills he was tired. It was so early he decided to sit down on the dewy grass and take a nap. Lying on his back he saw how deep and blue the sky was. By the sun he knew that Miss Olson would be at least an hour coming, so he closed his eyes and listened to squirrels chatter. So friendly it was, his eyes grew heavy. The next thing he knew he was awakened with a shake.

"Gypsy!"

"I came to warn you, Twm," said Gypsy breathless. "Benja be worse. An ambulance came for him this morning."

"Never."

"Aye, mun."

Twm felt a ball of fear rise in his stomach, and then he remembered why he was here in the dingle, and lying under the tree. He remembered the horror of the dark coal mine . . . could the teg help?

"Gypsy, remember I told you that perhaps a real teg would help me become all magic?" Twm said.

"Aye, but . . ."

"Well she is coming today, see. She must be on her way now. Supposed to be here by ten o'clock."

"It's ten-thirty now," said Gypsy doubtfully.

"Well, perhaps she got held up. Listen, you go up the tree and wait, and I will go and look around. Perhaps she got lost."

"Wait a bit, mun," replied Gypsy. "When will I know to come down, and who is she?"

"I'll whistle," said Twm. "I can't tell you who she is yet, but I will as soon as I know for sure she's a teg."

Twm trudged from one side of the dingle to the other, but no sight of Miss Olson. He waited and waited. "Oh no," he whispered, "she isn't coming."

With a heavy heart he walked towards the tree and whistled. Gypsy came down like a squirrel.

"Well, where is she?"

"I looked and looked, and waited and waited," said Twm. "Perhaps she forgot."

"Can't be much of a teg if she forgot."

"Perhaps she is trying to find the dingle, but I told her the way."

"Can't be much of a teg if she loses herself," reasoned Gypsy. "Did you ever see her wings?"

"No, she wears a frock, mun," Twm said shortly.

"Heisht!" called Gypsy. "I hear something."

Twm did too. Gypsy nimbly went up the tree again after Twm promised he would whistle for him. "But it doesn't sound like wings," whispered Gypsy from a topmost branch. "It sounds like feet. Lots of feet."

Gypsy was right. Over the rise of the hill came Miss Olson followed by six or eight girls. "Ugh!" hissed Gypsy.

"Heisht!" breathed Twm.

"Twm," called Miss Olson smiling brightly, "I met these girls on my way, and it's well I did. I would have surely gotten lost. They showed me the way. Now perhaps you will show all of us the dingle."

The girls giggled and Twm groaned, and wished with all his heart he was up the tree with Gypsy. How could he get rid of her and them? It came to Twm unmistakably that he had been wrong about Miss Olson. She was no teg. But how could he get rid of them? It would be worse still if Mortimer came, and the rest of the gang. Boyo, would they let him have it for bringing a teacher and a lot of girls to their place.

Twm would have welcomed even Proud Parry's gamekeeper just then.

That was it. If someway he could get the keeper to chase them away, then he and Gypsy could decide what they must do. Then again, perhaps Miss Olson was only making mischief with Twm. Perhaps she could fly all along and just needed the right situation to take flight. Perhaps if Proud Parry's gamekeeper chased her. Twm's imagination soared again in glorious optimism. It was a chance, but a chance Twm knew he must take.

"Well, what will we do?" Miss Olson asked.

"Would you like to see me catch a fish, miss?" Twm answered sweetly.

"Can you, Twm?"

"Aye. Come on, you will see," he said importantly.

He led the chattering group through the dingle, through the field, and around to the farther side where there were no-trespassing signs.

"Do you know," said Twm to keep them occupied, "that in olden times Prince Gwyddno Longshanks had a castle here and every May Day over a hundred fish were taken out of here."

Twm had his shoes off and was crawling through the weeds into the water and over the boulders to the pool where the big trouts slept. Steady . . . he peered at one that lay quietly in the shade.

"Careful, Twm."

"Heisht!" said Twm forgetting she was a teacher.

Nearer and nearer Twm went. He put his hand on the bottom sending up a screen of mud. He could feel the fish's tail against the palm of his hand . . . silly old fish. He was remembering what Gypsy told him. Wait until the breathing was right . . . open, close, open, close, closer, closer . . . get him. The stream swirled and foamed and Twm forgot everything but the fish.

"He's got him. He's got him," cried Miss Olson as Twm held on to the slipping, flapping, flying two-pounder. He threw the trout on the bank proudly. He stood there smiling, but only for a moment. A big hand fell on Twm's shoulder . . . two hands in fact: Proud Parry and his bailiff.

13

"FLY, MISS OLSON," Twm shouted. "Fly, fly, fly."

But she just stood there, her eyes going wide as the other children ran in all directions and Twm wriggled worse than a fish in the bailiff's grasp.

"Let go of that child," Miss Olson ordered.

Proud Parry made long strides to where she stood. "Your name, please," he said.

"I would like to know *your* name," she said rubbing her nose furiously. "And why you and that big bully are picking on a little boy."

"My name is Lord Bloyd Parry," he said. "And you are trespassing on my land."

She looked quickly at Twm, rubbed her nose some more and looked back at Proud Parry. "We weren't doing any harm."

"Just poaching my fish," said Parry.

"It's a well-known fact," she said, "that all little boys like to fish. Now in my country . . ."

Proud Parry lowered his eyelids as if a heavy wind were blowing. Twm dug his hands deep into his pockets and prayed that Miss Olson would be still. In books, he thought, the ground would open now and he would escape down a rabbit hole. If only he could. But no, Miss Olson kept on talking about democracy and rights and Parry was getting red as a strawberry. And the bailiff had a strangle hold on Twm.

"American, is it?" Parry was saying now. "No laws in America then?"

"I didn't say that," she snapped. "We are just kinder to children."

Twm trembled for her. No one blasted Parry like that. Parry would give six months in prison for a leg of rabbit. He would give a year for a trout, even if you didn't say anything but "yes sir, no sir."

"The very idea," she was saying, "the very idea, honestly! What an undemocratic attitude."

"Why are you in this very undemocratic land?" Parry asked quietly.

"I'm an exchange teacher," she said.

"Indeed," said Parry, "if this is what you are teaching the children, I will have to speak to the headmaster about it."

Miss Olson's face paled, but she stood her ground. "I'm

sure no headmaster would condone what you do to children . . . See how they all fled from you?''

Now she has done it, thought Twm. We will all go to jail. What more could he do wrong? Poaching fish, being responsible for Benja Bowen perhaps being killed. Why, they would put him in jail forever and ever . . . How could he get away? It was no use now trying to save Miss Olson. She had talked herself into prison. Perhaps he could kick the bailiff in the shin. Twm was thinking it over when all of a sudden the blacksmith's voice shattered the quiet hum of conversation between Proud Parry and Miss Olson.

''The bull is in the second field,'' he shouted. ''Someone left the gate open.''

Proud Parry turned sharp to the bailiff. ''Didn't you close the gate, man?''

''I came in a hurry when I saw this one,'' said the bailiff.

In the distance Twm could see the bull making for the lambing field. He measured the distance with his eyes. Could he head him off? He could jump over this fence . . . Yes, he had to do it. There wasn't a moment to lose. No time to stop and to think. Twm raced across the fields taking off his red jacket and waving it back and forth. The bull stopped dead and pawed the ground as though he were thinking it over.

Twm danced cautiously in front of him and through the gate, and the bull thundered towards him. But Twm darted to the gate and closed it just as the bull was about to come charging and bellowing through. And bellow he did when he caught his horns in the gate.

"Twm," screamed Miss Olson. "Twm, Twm, are you all right?"

"You young fool," called Proud Parry. "Come back here."

But Twm didn't wait to hear more. He ran swiftly through the woods until he came to the great oak tree. Then he was up on the topmost branch motioning to Gypsy to be quiet.

"I know," whispered Gypsy, "I got eyes."

They sat up there holding their breath while Miss Olson, Proud Parry, the bailiff and all the girls paraded up and down looking for Twm. The bailiff squinted up the tree and Twm was reminded of those newspaper picture puzzles. Find the two boys and an owl in this drawing of a tree. But the bailiff wasn't good at puzzles, for though he seemed to look straight through Twm and Gypsy, he didn't see them and soon moved on.

Twm felt numb with terror.

"Not much of a teg," said Gypsy.

"Aye."

"We will never be able to go back now with Benja so sick and Proud Parry hunting us. But we can stay here, Twm," he said cheerfully. "I've got a plan. We can live in this tree and no one will ever find us."

"We are not squirrels," said Twm. "How can we live in a tree?"

"Come on, I'll show you," said Gypsy.

Hidden away in a grove of trees was a wooden structure that Gypsy had nailed together from boxes and crates.

"I got these from the greengrocer shop," he explained, "and I've got lots of orange rope so we can bind it to the trunk of the tree. I've got some big nails, too."

"How can we get it up there?" Twm wanted to know.

"You'll see."

They carried the little house to the trunk of the tree. Then Gypsy lowered a lasso made of orange rope and they tied it through holes on opposite sides of the house. Twm and Gypsy gave a mighty heave and finally, inch by inch, the tree house went up. Then with more hammering with rocks and tying of orange rope to the tough vines, the tree house held. First it swayed this way and that until Twm felt giddy, but with more rope and more hammering it was secure.

"A real tree house," said Twm with wonder.

"Not yet," said Gypsy. "Let's cover it with branches." And soon it was covered in a sea of leaves.

"They'll never find us now," said Gypsy proudly. "No one but you and I know about this place."

Twm had to admit it was peaceful sitting in that tree. He didn't blame Gypsy for liking it up here away from teachers, parents and sticky pink girls.

After a while Gypsy suggested that they go for a swim.

"We better be careful," Twm said. "Proud Parry may be watching."

"Not him," said Gypsy. "I know what he is doing."

"What?"

"Having tea. You can set a clock by him, mun."

"And the bailiff and the Gwallter?"

"Same, same exactly . . . all having tea."

The river gleamed in the late afternoon sun. Twm and Gypsy made sure no one was around, took off their clothes and jumped into the water.

They gasped. It was colder than when Twm went in for the trout, but once they got used to it the river felt deliciously cool after their hard work. They pretended they were fish. They were eels, they were dead men floating. They were ships parting the waves with their prows. They felt no longing for the valley humming in the distance. At last Gypsy said they had better go and see about supper.

"You scared of traps, Twm?" Gypsy asked.

"No."

"Right then, follow me!" whispered Gypsy. "We will fox that old bailiff."

Away ran Gypsy and Twm to the burrows of the rabbits. "Wish I had my ferret," said Gypsy. "But tonight, uh, Twm?"

"Perhaps," said Twm. "Somehow I don't think my magic is working today."

"Easy now," warned Gypsy. "Under the fence and follow me, and watch out for traps. Your magic will come back tonight, wait and see, Twm. Now follow me easy, mun."

This was Gypsy's world and he knew it like his hand. "Look." He pointed to the trap. "Throw me a stick."

Twm saw the steel jaws of the trap gaping under the leaves, the spring curved tight and ready for a rabbit's foot. Gypsy swung the stick and the jaws slammed shut.

"If you ever got your foot in that, you would be sorry," he said to Twm. "See, here is another, but a rabbit is in this one. And here's another. Wish I had my ferret. You could set him down by a rabbit hole and see rabbits come out like a stream."

"Two rabbits," said Twm delightedly. "That will make a good supper."

"Aye, and tomorrow we will have hedgehog."

"That be Gypsy food."

"Aye, better than chicken. Did you ever have it cooked in balls of mud?"

"Never."

"Tomorrow you shall," Gypsy promised.

They made a fire of sticks and after Gypsy had cleaned the rabbits he cooked them over the fire. The smell was delicious. Gypsy was better than Twm's mam when it came to roasting rabbits on a spit. They ate them hot and soon Twm was as full as an egg.

"Just imagine, Twm, we can stay here forever."

"Forever?" Twm asked. "I wonder what they be thinking at home? I hope Mam doesn't cry too much."

"Women always cry too much," said Gypsy, spitting out more bones. "Even the widow cries basinsful, but she don't mean no harm, mind."

"Let's go hunting for hedgehogs," said Twm, wanting to stop talking about Mam and home.

"Wait till it's dark, mun."

"Gypsy, what will we do if we meet a bear?"

"Don't be daft. No bears here," said Gypsy. "Wild ponies, maybe, but no bears on this mountain. See, it is getting dark. In a few minutes we can get a hedgehog. Stay behind me and look out for traps."

Twm followed close behind Gypsy, treading on his heel, in fact.

"Och!" cried Gypsy. "Be careful, mun. Now remember what I said. Look out for traps, boyo, or you will be hopping your way up to the upper palace with Benja."

Twm wished with all his heart Gypsy hadn't mentioned Benja. He shuffled behind Gypsy, keeping his distance. Suddenly Gypsy stopped and pointed. "What's that?" whispered Twm. "It's a hedgehog, a hedgehog," he cried.

"Don't touch 'less you want a handful of spines."

"I know, I know," said Twm irritably. "I'm not a babby."

Twm watched sulkily as Gypsy rolled the hedgehog over

with no effort. The silly creature lay on his back not knowing what to do and Gypsy, quick as a wink, had the penknife out and the poor thing was dead.

"He'll make a good supper tomorrow," said Gypsy. In a few minutes he had the hedgehog cleaned and wrapped in a ball of clay. Then he wrapped the clay in fresh leaves and placed the hedgehog in a tree away from the thieving badgers.

"Now it is time to go and bring my ferret back to life," said Gypsy.

Twm was afraid of that. He sighed but he followed Gypsy.

"This is the place," said Gypsy eagerly. "The moon is just about as full as it can be, so the magic should work for you, Twm."

Gypsy dug and dug, but found no ferret. "I know he is here someplace," said Gypsy, frantically digging one hole after another until the ground looked like a mole colony. Twm was torn between gladness for himself, and sorrow for Gypsy.

"We better go now, Gypsy," he said gently. "The ferret isn't there, mun. He has gone to heaven. Can't you just see him in ferret heaven, Gypsy, going down rabbit holes, his nose up, sniffing for more than he can eat?"

"Aye, sending those rabbits out like a stream."

Then Gypsy bent down his head and cried and cried. And Twm had trouble swallowing.

"You will always be my friend, Twm?"

"Aye."

"Right then," said Gypsy between sniffs. "Now we go to bed. We must be up early in the morning."

Up in the tree house, Twm could see Gypsy's face glimmer white like candlelight. Twm thought he felt a drop of rain, but it was a bead of sweat slipping down his cheek. The tree gave an evil creak. Gypsy hissed to Twm not to move so quickly. And then the moon slipped behind a cloud and Twm shivered.

"What's the matter?" Gypsy asked. "You be shivering to make your bones loose, mun."

"Cold," answered Twm, "cold and dark." Twm was thinking of the coal mine again.

"This is your first time," said Gypsy kindly. And Twm blinked back the tears.

"It's dark and no one to see," said Gypsy taking Twm's hand in his. "I was afraid the first time, mind."

"You were? Gypsy, were you not afeared down in the coal mine?"

"No indeed. I think it would be fun down there."

Twm shivered again. Never, never, if he could help it, would he go down there again. But better not say, or Gypsy would think he was a babby.

"Where did you stay the first time you run away, Gypsy?"

"In a chicken house," he replied. "It was raining so fast fish could swim through it. Hens are warm old things on a rainy night. Gentle old women are hens, look you, unless there be a cockerel around. Cockerels be nasty birds," he said. "Crowing and telling people you be there. Aye, it wasn't bad in the henhouse. But I like the tree house best. Now we sleep, is it? Tomorrow we catch fish."

Not for the world would Twm admit the stillness and the dark of the night were making him afraid. He was ashamed of his fear and not brave enough to tell about it. He went to sleep holding fast to Gypsy's hand.

14

Twm awoke with a start. Gran must have put a block of wood under the feathers, was his first thought. But he looked through the doorway of the tree house and the stars were glinting through the leaves.

"Hey," said Twm. "Where am I?" He peered at the strange shape that was huddled at his feet. "Hey," he called again.

"Go back to sleep," said the voice.

"Gypsy," said Twm delightedly. "We are still here then."

"Don't need to advertise it," said Gypsy crossly. "Go back to sleep."

When Twm woke again it was mild and clear. The stream in the distance was a ribbon of shining blue water. The buttercups and daisies were twinkling in the fields and everything smelled new.

"Let's go fishing before breakfast," suggested Twm.

"We'll have to, mun," said Gypsy, "if we expect to eat. You don't have your mam baking her bread, you know."

Twm wished Gypsy hadn't mentioned his mother. He didn't want to think about her or anyone else connected with home. In spite of the beautiful morning, he felt uneasy. This running away was very different from skipping school. Then he had always known that he was going back. Now he was leaving his family, perhaps forever. He felt guilty about Miss Olson, too. If he hadn't been so afraid of going to prison because of Benja, he wouldn't have gotten her into all that trouble. But perhaps Parry would go easy with her because she was an American. If only she had been a teg, Gypsy and he could be flying now with the larks.

"Come on, mun," said Gypsy. "By the sun it must be five o'clock. It won't be safe to go fishing soon."

The boys left the tree and made their way down to the stream. It was calm and silent.

They pulled off their clothes and hopped quietly into the cold water, afraid of waking any of Parry's servants.

"I hope Parry is snoring his way up to heaven," said Gypsy. They paddled in the water, then leaped from rock to rock. "Now remember what I told you," said Gypsy. "Crook the fingers around the gills, heave up and throw him wide . . . but listen to the breathing."

Twm watched Gypsy get a fish in a matter of minutes, it

seemed. He stood there grinning with a fish, two pounds if he was an ounce. "Now you," whispered Gypsy.

Twm bit back a gasp as the river flooded him all over. He crawled through the reeds to the deep part of the stream.

"Come on, boyo," said Twm under his breath. "It's cold." He shivered with joy though when he felt the belly of the fish. Open, close, open, close . . . got him. No. The trout leaped against the green-blue water and was gone.

"I told you to wait," said Gypsy impatiently. "You'll never learn to fish at this rate."

"I caught a bigger one yesterday than you ever had," Twm retorted.

"You must have been lucky," said Gypsy scornfully.

"I'll show you," said Twm setting his lip.

In he went again. This time he waited, and waited and waited, until the daft old fish came towards his hand. It felt like his hand was turning blue, but still Twm waited and stroked the fish under the gills—one, two, one, two, one, two . . . "Got him. Got him."

"Will you heisht," hissed Gypsy. "You'll wake up the whole valley. It's a fair-looking fish," he admitted.

"It's bigger than yours," said Twm.

"It is not."

"It is."

"I'll get another one," said Gypsy, stowing his fish high in a tree away from the otters.

And he was in the water again, whispering, "I've the biggest one in the world. It's a grancher salmon, look you."

The fishing spirit had taken the two boys. Breakfast was forgotten. Food didn't seem important. They were fishing, body and soul . . . bass, salmon, trout. "Wish my father—"

Twm stopped. He did not want to think about his father.

"Come on," said Gypsy happily. "We'd better stop now and cook breakfast."

They came back to their new home glad-hearted and hungry. Gypsy soon had a fire going, and sizzling over the flames was the trout, its silver coat turning deep brown. No fish ever tasted so good to Twm before.

"It's because we cooked it quickly," said Gypsy. "Fresh fish always tastes better cooked quickly as soon as it leaves the water."

Now the two boys rested in the shade. The larks were diving about them and Twm wished again that he might fly. To be up there diving and soaring in the crystal clear of the white and blue of the sky.

"Poor Benja," he said to Gypsy. "He might be dead and here we are having fun."

"If he is, we can't help him," said Gypsy, "and he could make it bad for us."

"It's all our fault," cried Twm, suddenly filled with remorse. He had pushed the guilty feeling down and down and down but it bubbled up. Suddenly he wanted to go home, confess, take his punishment and get it over with. He told Gypsy so.

"You can't, mun," said Gypsy in alarm.

"They may go easy with us since it's the first time."

"For you perhaps," said Gypsy. "The widow told me if I ever got in trouble again, she would send me back to the workhouse."

"Let's go back," urged Twm. "It always goes easier if you give yourself up."

"All right," said Gypsy. "But not yet. We might as well finish the day up. We won't get into any more trouble if we finish the day and there's so much to do."

"All right," agreed Twm, "but back for supper, mind."

"Remember," said Gypsy, "they'll keep up a special watch on us after this. So let's make this a day we'll never forget."

They did. They found some pheasant eggs and feasted on them for lunch. They played pirates and robbers and Welsh and English. They told riddles, fried more fish and cooked another rabbit, and the day went faster than any that Twm had ever known.

But it went, and as the sun began to set behind the tump, Twm reminded Gypsy that they must go back. "They must be looking for us," he said.

"They were last night," said Gypsy.

"What!" said Twm.

137

"I heard them pass right under the tree," said Gypsy. "So I thought I'd keep quiet. Your father was there. He thinks we be lost in the mines."

"Well, I'm going home," said Twm. "My poor father. How could you do such a thing!"

"Aw, Twm," said Gypsy. "You can't go home yet."

"Yes I can."

"We only got here yesterday, mun."

"I'm going home," said Twm stubbornly.

"Let's go for a swim first."

"I'm going, Gypsy," he said tying his shoes.

"Babby," shouted Gypsy. "Big babby. Go home and your mother will warm up the bottle."

"Do you want to fight?" asked Twm putting up his fist.

"Righto," said Gypsy standing upright.

The mountain grass was against Twm's back with the blow of Gypsy's fist. He stared at the stars, shook his head and was on his feet, fast. Now they were a pair of bantams, fists flying and noses bleeding. Soon they were both panting on the grass.

"You still going home?" said Gypsy.

"Aye, Gypsy. I have been thinking if we get caught, and we are sure to be, it's going to be hard on us. Perhaps they won't let us back into school, mun. Perhaps they will send us straight down the mines. I don't want to go down there, Gypsy. And Dada says school is the one way to not go into the coal mines. I'm going back home and back to school."

"Righto," said Gypsy, wistful now. "Tell the widow I'm sorry, but I'm not coming back."

"Why, Gypsy?" asked Twm, his heart going heavy at the sight of Gypsy's face.

"This is my home now, Twm," he said simply. "The widow will be glad to see the end of me."

"What's that?" said Twm as a flash of lightning streaked across the sky.

"A storm," said Gypsy. "We better go into the tree house until it stops. Sopping you will be if it rains."

No sooner had Gypsy spoken than a deep angry roar of thunder tumbled and rumbled through the heavens. Now big raindrops were falling.

"The tree house," urged Gypsy.

Up they climbed, hanging on to the rungs of wet bark and plunging into the house that shook and creaked in the sullen night. One blinding flash followed another and bolt after bolt of thunder clapped.

"Look," shouted Twm, "it's leaking."

The rain was pouring in through the sodden crates as though from a water tap. Gypsy stood there for a moment watching his house being destroyed.

"All right," he said. "We have to run for it, boyo."

Down the tree they were running and shouting and splashing their way seizing each other's hand as they tumbled and fell down the mountain path to the valley below.

When they arrived at the corner of their street, every little stone house looked newly washed. The chimney pots glistened and steamy smoke was curling out of them.

"I wonder if they had supper," said Twm.

"We'll soon see," said Gypsy. "Well, so long."

"Wait," said Twm. "Let's go to your house first. If we go together perhaps they will not be so hard on us."

"That's right," said Gypsy. "The widow never gives it to me if someone is around."

But the widow's greengrocer shop was empty. They tip-toed around, found some custard in the pantry, stirred up the coal fire and played with the tiger cat, but still the widow didn't appear.

"Well then," said Twm regretfully, "we had better go to my house."

They walked up the street to Twm's house, braver than they felt, and too soon found themselves in Twm's backyard. They peered into the kitchen window. There sat Twm's mother, Gran, Morfydd and the widow, talking.

"Like my own flesh and blood was Gypsy. A lovely boy, my lovely boy. Where is my boy . . . I'm sorry," the widow said with tears streaming down her cheeks. "Where is he?"

"Here we are," said Twm pushing Gypsy into the kitchen.

"What in the world?" said Gran. "You are going to get it, boyo, when your father gets home."

"Hush, Mother," said Twm's mam, rushing to Twm and taking him in her arms.

Gypsy smirked but not for long. The widow was kissing him one minute and scolding him the next.

"We thought you were both lost in the pit," said his mam. "The whole valley has been looking for you. Your father is out now and Grancher . . . Oh Twm, Twm, Twm, you are all right."

"Aye, mun," said Twm, glad they wanted him back but wishing that they would stop the sissy kissing.

"Was it all Miss Olson's fault?" Morfydd wanted to know.

"No," said Twm, " 'course not."

"It wasn't?" Morfydd said.

"No, who said it was?"

"Gran."

"What?"

"I did my duty," said Gran rubbing Twm down with a towel. "Frightened to death we all were when you didn't come home. I was sure that woman had bewitched you, but they wouldn't believe me."

"I should hope not," said Twm indignantly.

"Twm," said his mother seriously, "because of you and Gypsy, Miss Olson is in trouble. She was dismissed."

"What!"

"Yes, thanks to Gran and the widow, the whole town is

saying that she is a witch. Yes, and with Proud Parry and the school board she is in trouble. Why some people even say she was responsible for Benja, too. I think it's terrible to treat the poor woman this way."

"I just did my duty," said Gran.

"That's the last secret I ever tell you," said Twm hotly. "After you crossed your eyes and all."

"Come on, Gypsy," said the widow recovering herself. "Good night, Mrs. Tybach," said she to Gran. "You did right. It was your duty to get rid of that witch."

"Will you two stop it instantly," said Twm's mother. "Haven't you caused enough sorrow for the teacher?" She turned to Twm and held him close. "And Twm, you have filled him full of witches and nonsense since he was born. It has got to stop. Twm love, now you go to bed like a good boy."

Twm was too tired to argue. He did not see his father or Grancher that night. When they came home tired and worried, Dada's first reaction to the news of Twm was joy. Grancher started to do a jig. But he was stopped in mid-jig by Gran, who said she wasn't going to stay another day in this house to be insulted by her daughter-in-law.

Dada said that asleep or not Twm should be awakened for a good thrashing.

"Don't you dare wake him, now," said Mam. "It's your

own mother's fault filling him full of this nonsense. I won't have it. I won't have it."

"Please, Tessa," said Dada. "Not in front of Morfydd. She can see plenty of fighting outside."

"To bed, Morfydd," snapped Mam.

Twm was snuggled between the soft cotton blankets and warm feathers while the blasting, sniffling, the threats and promises were going on downstairs. Tomorrow was another day, and one that Twm was not likely ever to forget.

15

Twm's father presented Twm before Proud Parry. Twm had never been in the mansion house before. He shivered when his father rang the bell and would have run away when the surprised footman answered it if his father hadn't had him by the collar.

"We want to see Lord Parry," said Twm's father quietly.

"He's a busy man, a busy man," said the footman. "What do you want?"

"We have come about the poaching," said Twm's father. "Away, man, to him. He will see us," he said firmly.

"Very well," snapped the footman. "Wipe your feet on the mat, please." He led them importantly down a marble hall, knocked at a high white door, and when Parry's voice said "Come in," Twm's heart jumped inside him.

The big door opened. Silently, Twm and his father walked

into the crimson-carpeted room. In front of the big desk stood Gypsy and the widow.

Twm didn't look at Gypsy. He kept his eyes riveted on the big fireplace where a whole log sputtered on the hearth. Lord Parry motioned Twm's father and the widow into chairs the color of moss. Standing there Twm forgot to be frightened for the room was so beautiful. Curtains as pale and green as lettuce hung from floor to ceiling at the big window that overlooked the meadows. Big leather books lined the walls. There's riches, Twm thought. He was brought back with a start when Proud Parry thundered, "Well, what are we going to do with these boys?"

"That's what I came about, sir," said Twm's father respectfully.

"Same, same exactly," said the widow.

"What do you have to say for yourself, Twm?" said Parry in an awful voice.

Twm hung his head.

"Twm, why did you take that teacher into my land?" thundered Parry.

"I was trying to get rid of all the girls," Twm said. "See, I thought that if I could just get rid of the girls, Miss Olson would teach me how to fly."

"What?"

"He thought she was a teg, sir," Twm's father explained. "She has blond hair, see."

This had a terrible effect on Proud Parry. He went double, got out his handkerchief and blew his nose like a trumpet. "I see," he said at last, "but that doesn't explain why they were on my land."

"I wanted you and your bailiff to chase the girls away," Twm said. "That was the only reason. I thought that was the only way to get rid of them. And after, I thought, I thought . . ."

"The teg would teach you how to fly all over my land, help yourself to my game and have a fine time for yourselves. Well, isn't that what you thought?" he asked, his bushy eyebrows coming together like giant caterpillars. He looked at Twm and he looked at Gypsy and he swished his thin whip against his breeches. He said finally, "What shall we do with them, Mr. Tybach?"

"Anything you like, sir."

Twm closed his eyes while he awaited sentence. Six months on bread and water was the least he would get.

"If you will permit me, sir," Twm heard his father say, "I will see that Twm is punished so that he never poaches on your land again."

Twm breathed a sigh of relief.

"And Gypsy," said Parry.

"I'll take whatever Twm takes," said Gypsy.

"You certainly will," said the widow.

"Good boyo," Twm said under his breath.

"Right then," said Proud Parry, "see that they do. I'm more sorry than I can say for that young American teacher."

"Aye, it wasn't her fault, sir," said Twm, desperately wanting to tell all. "She didn't know it was posted, see."

"No she didn't, sir," said his father.

"And she didn't know that these young scamps have poached my salmon, or taken my rabbits out of the traps?"

"And she didn't know about the hedgehog either," said Twm reveling in his confession.

"I reported her to the school board," said Parry. "There's sorry I am for that. But how was I to know?"

"Aye, pity," said Dada. "A hard time she has had in the valley." He glared at the widow. "The old ones are saying that she is a witch bent on destroying the valley and our young, and I heard tell that the school board is saying she set education back more than when the English came to Wales. I'm sorry for her, I can tell you."

"Yes, yes, yes," said Parry . . . "Pity, pity, pity."

"Well, I don't feel sorry for her," said the widow. "Strange ideas she's been putting in their heads, when all they need is plenty of cane and discipline, now."

"I think you should know," said Twm's father sternly, "that my mother has already apologized to Miss Olson. And if I had my way, the whole valley would make a public apology. The very idea, saying that she was responsible for Benja going into the coal mine, that she bewitched him, the very idea!''

"I was the one who got Benja into trouble," said Twm. "And I took him to tease the blacksmith, and I took him to the coal trams," said Twm who felt that if he was going to have to be punished, he wanted it all at once.

"I dared Benja, too," said Gypsy not to be outdone. "And I showed Twm how to poach, and how to fish, and I built the tree house that no one could find, and I showed him how to spring traps, skin a hedgehog . . .''

"Enough!" thundered Proud Parry and he leaned back as if he were exhausted.

"Well, good day to you, sir," said Twm's father, taking a firm hold of Twm who was about to go into more confessing.

"I don't know what to do about these two," Proud Parry was saying.

"Don't worry, we will take care of them," said Dada backing out and bowing to Parry.

"Right then," said Parry, "I'm so sorry about the teacher. We have been unfair."

"Now you two get yourselves to school," said Dada, "and Twm, I want you home early."

"Aye, Dada."

Twm and Gypsy were trudging up the hill now in silence.

Finally Gypsy said: "Now we are going to get it, boyo. There is a daft old thing you are to tell all."

"Aye, you did too, Gypsy."

"I wonder what our punishment will be? I wish your father had passed sentence right away. I don't fancy waiting," Gypsy grumbled. "It will be rough with us, boyo."

"Well, the gang will be glad to see us," Twm said. But they were not happy to see them at all.

"Look what you did," cried Mortimer. "You lost us the best teacher the school ever had."

"You called her barmy," shouted Twm.

"I've a good mind to punch you," sputtered Mortimer.

"Try it, just try it," said Twm holding up his fists. "Go on with you, Mortimer snortimer, take your babby gang with you."

"Not me, Twm," said Benja quietly. He came up to Twm wearing a bandage bigger than a pudding cover. "I didn't blab, Twm. I kept my oath."

"Benja!" cried Twm. "You be all right?"

"Aye, mun, right as rain."

"They took you to the hospital, mun."

"Just to have X rays on my head. But no bones broken, see, just a bruise inside my head that made me sleepy. Want a piece of Welsh butter taffy?" he asked casually.

"What about me, Benja?" asked Mortimer.

"Ah, go on, Mortimer snortimer," cried Benja. "You never wanted me in your gang. And I don't want to be 'less Twm and Gypsy be in it, too."

Mortimer looked threateningly at Benja, who stepped back behind Gypsy and Twm. They stood there glaring. Mortimer looked from one to the other, spat on the floor and walked away towards the gang.

"You and Gypsy be better than all of them," said Benja warmly. And he walked between them. Twm said: "Oh, go on with you, Benja," but he was warmed by Benja's words.

Once they were in school, though, Miss Davies sprang at Twm and Gypsy and told them to go straight to the headmaster's office. "You should be ashamed, ashamed," she cried, "causing all this trouble, this trouble."

And then it was the headmaster. The headmaster received them with a roar. His eyes flashed first at Gypsy then Twm: "Well, what do you have to say for yourself? Tell me that?" But before Twm could open his mouth the schoolmaster thundered, "You are a disgrace to the school and the valley. You have made us all look bad in the American's eyes."

"I did all that?" asked Twm.

"Sorry," mumbled Gypsy.

"Yes, she was doing well, learning our ways, and then . . . and then this. This disgrace. Put out your hands, both of you."

Twm felt the terrible pain as the stick came down on his hand six times.

"Simple you made us all look," said the headmaster furiously. "Now Proud Parry blames the school board."

Swish, swish went the stick. Blindly Twm bore the pain, but tears were coming.

"Now go to your room both of you and this is little to what you will get if I have trouble with you again. Now go."

"Sit down," snapped Miss Davies. "Thanks to you I have to teach this class again. Now get to work and I want to see if those hen brains are oiled this morning."

As Twm sat rubbing his burning hands under the beady eye of Miss Davies, he wondered whatever had possessed him to make him leave that tree house paradise to listen to the chanting of "Twelve inches is a foot, three feet is a yard, fourteen pounds in a stone, twelve stone in a hundred weight, twice two are four, one God is love, one Lord is king"; so it would be forever and ever. Aye, this was punishment all right. Could the mines be worse?

How Twm longed for Miss Olson. He didn't care that she wasn't a witch or a teg. He liked her anyway. How he missed her bright talk about America and twenty-eight flavors of ice cream. He looked over at Gypsy. What trouble they were both in. Would he ever see Miss Olson again? Would there be any point to seeing her? Words are useless things in a lost friendship.

He slumped again in his desk. Witch or no, she was the best teacher they had ever had. With her help he could learn. It seemed more like fun than learning when she told him things.

Yet it might be worse, he decided. There was still the festival on Monday, only days away now. Would Gypsy find his tribe among the hurdy-gurdies? Would his dada win the prize for the best poem set to music? Twm knew it by heart now, and sung it over in his mind.

Listen to the moon-wind
Hummin' autumn wild.
Sleep, little honey thing!
Dream, little child!

Listen to the sigh-sound
Sobbin' through the night.
Rest you, little honey thing.
Close your eyes tight.

Listen to the moon-wind
Shuffle on the stairs . . .

"Twm Tybach, will you open your history book and stop your everlasting dreaming?" shouted Miss Davies. "Silent reading, and you will all be tested, so pay attention."

But Twm's mind was on the festival. It would last a whole day, almost forever. Pity Miss Olson would miss it. Well, he had done his best, and Gypsy too, mind. They had confessed like men. And always Twm would remember her in his prayers. God would take care of Miss Olson. God knew he was sorry for all the trouble he caused her.

With relief, Twm put away his books after the school day was done. Nothing more can happen today, he was convinced. But as he was going out the door Miss Davies pointed to him.

"Yes, miss," Twm said timidly.

"You have lost your part in the pageant," she said shortly. "I'm sure you must know that . . . must know that. But in case you didn't, I'm telling you. You lost your part . . . lost your part."

Twm walked home wondering if God knew how hard life was for him.

"Aye, boyo," said his father later that night. "There is little that God does not know."

Twm's dad had requested that the kitchen be empty so he could talk with Twm.

"Hard day, boyo?" he asked.

"Aye, Dada, middling hard." Twm blinked back the tears.

"You haven't had my punishment yet, Twm."

"Aye," he agreed. "Is that why the kitchen is empty?"

"No . . . I'll tell you when, never fear. You look as if you had enough for one day. But I'm not forgetting, mind."

Twm wished he would get it over, but didn't want to

press. "I hope it will be a good day for the festival," he said conversationally.

"Aye."

"Your poem is sure to win."

"Twm, what are we going to do with you?" he said sadly.

"I'm doing better in school, or was, Dada. I lost my part in the pageant."

"You have your head full of tegs," Dada said. "That's what has gotten you into all this. There's sad Grancher will be to hear you've lost the part."

"So does Gran believe in tegs," Twm said.

"Twm, Gran never had any schooling. She worked on top of the pit when she was twelve. Dreaming about tegs was the one way she could forget about the coal dust. But you have a chance to get away from the pit. And this is your last chance, boyo. Can't you see that?"

"Is Grancher still angry with Gran?" Twm asked, dying to shift the conversation from himself.

"No. They have gone to a Bible meeting. Perhaps the good preacher can convince Gran that God is more important than tegs. Perhaps she will believe him."

"She believes in both God and tegs."

"Twm, boy, there are no tegs."

"Dada! You don't believe that there are any tegs at all?"

"I know there aren't, boy. Oh, I believed once like you,

boyo. I believed there was an easy way of getting what you wanted out of life."

"When did you find out?"

"In the coal mines, Twm. Do you know why we wear buckles under our knees?"

"No . . . yes, to keep the small coal from getting through."

"Aye, and the rats from getting up."

Twm shivered. "You didn't get what you wanted out of life?"

"No, Twm. Give me my life over and I would do anything to stay out of the mines. It is not good down there."

"I know, Dada . . . I know. It is black as pitch and smells awful."

"Aye, but I'm in coal for life, son. I missed my chance in school. But you have a chance to get out. Through book learning, mind though, not tegs. I have a dream that one day you and your sister will come up our street wearing a college scarf. But you have to do your part, boyo."

"Aye, Dada. I'm doing better." Twm watched his father —the gray of his face, the eyes rimmed with coal that no amount of washing would take away. From time to time he coughed the miner's cough, and Twm lowered his head to hide the sorrow in his eyes. It seemed strange to see his dada this way, to hear him talk like this. Twm had always stood in awe of him, looked far up to him, and wanted to be a miner just like him. But after seeing the mine he knew what his father said was true as the Bible. The coal mine was a bad place for anyone to work.

"And I'll try harder, Dada. Even if I have to go into the mine I will do a good job," he promised. "And I won't mind," he lied.

"It might come to that, boyo. Even with a scholarship, it will take money."

"Don't worry, Dada. I will do a good job, and work hard," he said. "I just wish I could like school as our Morfydd does," he said regretfully. "Did you like school?"

"Never," said Dada, "until I left school forever. Then I would have given anything to go back. The one thing I got out of school was a love of poetry."

"Miss Davies said the mines are full of bards and singers," Twm said.

"Aye, Miss Davies is right. Will you do better in school, Twm?" asked his father searching Twm's face with his blue eyes.

"I'll try. I might like school better in time," said Twm grudgingly. "I will do better."

"God's way is the long hard way, Twm. Magic sounds quick and easy. Even the people who believe in tegs don't trust them. Better go to bed now, Twm. That's enough talk for to-night."

16

Twm awoke on festival morning to a dazzling blue day, and the air through his window was sparkling with the scents of spring.

There was plenty of activity downstairs, and no need, that holiday morning, for anyone to be shouted down to breakfast, what with Mam's and Gran's clattering of pots, Grancher's singing and Morfydd's giggling.

Twm couldn't help but be looking forward to roaming Proud Parry's land with no bailiff to give chase. And Dada had not said a single word more about punishment. Twm had thought that he would lose his penny allowance. But Saturday had come and gone and he was given a penny without a word. Twm knew his father hadn't forgotten, but perhaps he had felt that schoolmaster Evans's cane and Proud Parry and losing his part in the pageant all in one day was punishment enough. Twm heartily agreed.

Mam was dressed like a prize chicken, and Gran wore her cherried hat. The widow greengrocer was sitting at the table in a hat of feathers and moths. Grancher was night and day in a suit of twilight blue with strips of gold and spangles of silver paper, his bald head shining like glass. Morfydd danced around him in her queen's dress of curtains trimmed with white rabbit and pearl buttons. Gran and Twm's mother had been stitching for weeks. Dada was Robin Hood.

And what a scramble on the street, with the boys washed like colliers on a Saturday night and the girls frizzed and blossoming in their ribboned dresses. There were beards, bootblack faces, false noses and wigs.

To think I might have been king of the tegs, Twm considered regretfully. But he knew better than to mention it. Anyway, he didn't mind as long as he was there at the pageant.

"Twm," said his father. "Don't bother changing. You are not going to the festival. This is your punishment."

Twm stood unbelieving. This was his punishment. The worst punishment in the world. Worse than the schoolmaster's cane, worse than seeing Proud Parry. To be left alone on the biggest holiday of the year was terrible, terrible. Could six months of bread and water be worse? Twm doubted it.

"Please let me go," Twm pleaded. "I'll never do it again. Never, never."

"I'm sorry, Twm," said his father. "But I want to make

sure you remember what you did. What you did to your mother, to Miss Olson and to all of us. And it would please me very much if you would go and apologize to that teacher. She is all alone with strangers who have not been kind."

"I'm sure he's sorry," said Morfydd, appalled at the severe punishment.

"Silence," said Dada. And Twm knew it would do no good to complain.

And then he was alone. Twm watched the window while the procession passed. Never would he have believed that his very own father could be so cruel! Even his mother's tender kiss did not sweep away any of Twm's low spirits. In that dark moment he felt very sorry for Miss Olson, alone in the valley with no family, thousands of miles from home. But she was lucky she was going back to America in a few days. I wish I could go with her, thought Twm.

A knock on the door brought him up short. His heart leaped. Dada had relented. He could go after all. No, why would his father knock?

Twm hurried to the door. It was Gypsy Joe.

"Come on, Twm," he said. "We can see it all from the tree."

"I can't go," said Twm.

"Same, same exactly," said Gypsy. "I'm supposed to watch the shop. But I ask you, who will be buying vegetables to-day?"

For one wild moment Twm decided to go with Gypsy. No one would know. They could get back before the others and . . .

But his father's stern face came between him and his desire. What if they were caught? What would the punishment be then?

"No, Gypsy," said Twm virtuously. "I'm going to take my punishment like a man."

"Then you are simple," said Gypsy. "Simple and barmy."

"Not simple enough to get into trouble again, Gypsy. My father said I'm getting too old for such nonsense. I'm tired of always being in trouble." And it came suddenly to Twm that this was God's way to make him pay for what he had done to the American teacher. He wouldn't have to worry about paying any more.

"Aye," said Gypsy. "I said I would take what you took. I'll stay."

"Thank you, Gypsy," said Twm gratefully. He didn't have to be alone, after all. An idea suddenly came to him. Why not go and see Miss Olson? She was alone and they were alone and perhaps she could think of something interesting to tell them of America. Yes, and he would please his father, too, by going to see her.

Gypsy argued about going. But Twm talked and talked and soon they were locking up the greengrocery shop and on their way to the house where Miss Olson was staying.

"Why, boys," she said in pleasant surprise. "It was so nice for you to come and say goodbye."

"I'm sorry that you are going, miss," said Twm. "It's all my fault, isn't it? I didn't mean to get you into trouble."

"I know, Twm, your father told me. You thought I could teach you how to fly."

"Aye, but my father says there are no such things as tegs."

"Perhaps not," she replied. "But there is a way to learn how to fly."

"I tried," said Twm hotly, "but I fell on my nose."

"No, no, Twm, it's through books that you can learn. Through books you can do almost anything."

"Birds don't read books," said Gypsy.

"No, but books can save you from the coal mines," said Twm.

"They certainly can, Twm. The best of the world is in books, all waiting for you to learn. Why the first person who invented an airplane must have felt as you do, Twm."

"And they made wings instead of growing them."

"They certainly did," said Miss Olson. "They looked beyond their noses. What did you think lay beyond the mountains until you went to school?"

"I never thought about it," said Twm.

"Neither does a fish. A fish in the sea thinks that the world is all water. A lion in a jungle thinks the world is all jungle. Do you understand, Twm?"

"Aye, I'm going to work hard in school and learn how to make wings."

"I think that's simple," said Gypsy. "I would rather live in a caravan with my tribe."

"If you go on the way you have been going, Gypsy, you will end up in the coal mines," said Twm.

"Well, enough lectures," said Miss Olson. "Let's have a party. I have cake and apples and honey."

"And ginger beer," said Gypsy.

"I'm afraid I don't have any ginger beer. But we have tea or milk. I'll go put the kettle on."

A knock came on the door.

"So many visitors today," said Miss Olson.

"I hope they don't stay," Twm whispered to Gypsy. "I'm just beginning to have a good time."

"Me, too," said Gypsy. "To heck with the old festival."

Miss Olson came back into the room pink-faced. And who should follow her? No other than Proud Parry himself.

Twm and Gypsy jumped to their feet. "Goodbye, Miss Olson," said Twm.

"We'll be going," said Gypsy.

"You don't have to leave," said Miss Olson. "Lord Parry is staying only a moment."

Gypsy and Twm wasted no time getting into the hall. "Come on," said Gypsy. "Let's get away from here."

"Wait," said Twm. "Perhaps she is in trouble; wonder what she has done now?"

"Come on," said Gypsy.

But Twm listened at the open door. He motioned to Gypsy to come and listen, too. The two boys stood there staring at one another unbelievingly. Was that Proud Parry talking? Never.

"I want you to know, Miss Olson," he was saying, "that most of the teachers, parents of the children and myself are sorry to see you leave. Perhaps we did not treat you kindly. We Welsh don't take to strangers that way. I did not know until that young scamp told me, that you were not responsible for trespassing in my woods. You said nothing and I naturally assumed . . ."

"That's quite all right, Lord Parry," she said.

"Furthermore," he continued—and though he was apologizing it still sounded like a lecture, "I would like you to stay and finish the year."

"So would we," said Twm completely forgetting he shouldn't eavesdrop.

"Please stay, Miss Olson," begged Twm. "Then you can teach us so many things about flying planes, about history, and teach me things so that I'll never have to go into the coal mines . . ." He stopped for a breath.

By now Miss Olson was blushing red as a strawberry and Lord Parry looked confused.

"I can't afford not to accept such kindness," said Miss Olson. "But what about the schoolmaster?"

"Don't worry about a thing," said Lord Parry. "Well now, since that is settled, let us go and see what they are doing at the festival."

"We can't," said Twm regretfully. "We are being punished."

"And so you should be. Well, come along and I will explain to your father that this is a special occasion," said Lord Parry.

"He doesn't change his mind about punishments," said Twm. "But we will never poach again, will we, Gypsy?" he said earnestly.

"Well, come on anyway and you two reformed poachers can wait in my car while I speak to your parents."

"Don't tell the widow I left the shop, please," said Gypsy.

"If you tell my father I said 'sorry' to Miss Olson it might help," suggested Twm.

Into the big black car went Gypsy and Twm. They sat down quiet as mice on the gray plush seats. "Even if we can't stay," whispered Twm, "we have a ride in Parry's car."

Coming to the festival when it was in full swing was the most exciting thing ever. The crowd parted before them when the big black car drove into the grounds. Twm and Gypsy and Miss Olson waited while Proud Parry presented himself to Twm's father and the widow. They waited and waited.

"I knew it wouldn't do any good," said Twm after ten minutes had passed. "Dada never changes his mind."

At last Proud Parry returned with Twm's mother and father, Gran and Grancher.

"Twm," said his dada sternly, "I told you to stay home."

"I'm going," said Twm getting up.

"Please, Mr. Tybach, won't you reconsider?" begged Miss Olson. "Twm is honestly sorry. I have had a long talk with him and he is determined to do better."

Dada made a thin line with his lips. Twm knew that sign. No use begging. Better go.

"You said it was a pity he couldn't sing the chorus of your song," said Grancher.

"Aye, nobody can sing it better than Twm," Gran said.

"Twm has promised to do better in school, and I know he will," said Miss Olson.

"I will if you stay," said Twm.

"Silence!" roared Twm's father. Then he turned to Miss Olson with a lovely smile and Twm's heart soared. Perhaps, perhaps . . .

"Does this mean you will be staying on, Miss Olson?" Dada asked.

"Well . . ."

"Please, Miss Olson," Twm begged. "I'll be good as gold."

"Quiet, Twm," said his father.

"Well, Miss Olson?" said Proud Parry.

"Please, Miss Olson," said Gypsy. "Then they will let us stay at the festival."

"And mind you behave yourself," said the widow, pointing her green umbrella.

"Well, now you worked things very well for yourself, you young teg, you," Gran whispered.

Twm just grinned. Inside he was suddenly so happy he wanted to jump up and down and laugh out loud just for the sake of laughing. Miss Olson was going to stay, she was going to stay. With Miss Olson he could learn, because she made learning fun even though she wasn't a teg. And Dada said that through learning he would stay out of the coal mines and go far. Someday Twm would come up the street with a college scarf around his neck, and Mam would cry with happiness, and Dada would be so proud. Life was just wonderful by itself. There was no need for tegs.

Suddenly there was a roll of drums and a man with a trumpet was telling people to go into the big tent for the crowning of the bard. Time for Dada's song. Twm's knees felt like water. "Please, God, let my dada win," he prayed.

But once inside the tent he was dismayed to see his dada was listed last. He picked out his father and mother sitting among the competitors. Mam would play the harp. Morfydd was chattering with girls around her, looking cheerful and confident. But Twm sat silent and alert, knowing even now that Dada was not completely happy with his song.

"I wish they would hurry," said Gypsy. "I want to go on the roundabouts."

"Heisht," said Twm.

"Well, why don't they hurry?" demanded Gypsy.

The tent filled rapidly, and the five judges filed in to chairs reserved for them. The buzz of talk faded to an expectant hush.

Then the first competitor received such an applause that Twm sank back in his seat, soaked in misery. He watched the judges scribbling countless notes and talking together. Twm wondered if they would have anything else to say when Dada's turn came. He was shivering with anxiety by the time Mam and Dada took their place on stage.

"Let them win. Oh, please let them win, if only they come in second." He clenched his fist until his nails dug into his palms.

His father held up his hand and said: "I would like my son, Twm, to sing this. It was written for a soprano and I'm a countertenor."

Twm never knew how he reached the stage. Mam's first notes of accompaniment sounded and Twm's voice soared into song, winging across the tent—as Grancher said after, "winging right up to the windowsills of heaven"—until the final note died away and the applause roared in his ears.

Twm left the stage and sank down in his seat in confusion.

He only knew Dada was smiling, and Mam, Gran and Grancher were coming a little wet around the eyes. And then he saw Miss Olson and the judges smiling, too. It hadn't been too bad then?

After a brief consultation one of the judges stepped on the stage and an instant hush fell over the tent.

"Ladies and gentlemen, we have found the song we hoped to find here at the festival, and we have great pleasure in awarding to Mr. Twm Tybach the prize and crowning him bard."

Everyone was clapping now and cheering and drumming on the floor. Dada went up and the crown was placed on his head. Twm's heart was hammering so he could scarcely breathe as Dada said most of the applause belonged to Twm. He found it almost impossible to believe that he had somehow helped to bring this great honor to the family.

At last he and Gypsy were outside the tent. There stood the carnival in all its glory. So much to see and do.

There were still the three-legged race and the potato race to run. Then the coconut shells . . . *whizz, whirl* went the coconuts as the fattest man in the valley called "Roll a bowl a ball!" They joined Mortimer, Gerwin, Willy, and Benja on the roundabouts. Shoulder to shoulder they were on the bright-colored horses, tousled and crimson and standing up against the rules. Then it was the swing boats skimming to and fro, upside and down, right to the stars.

If it could only just last forever, thought Twm. Forever and ever, amen.

"Come on," a man shouted. "The dance ring is starting."

There was dancing to the fiddle now, with bright stockings going up in a trill of Welsh lace petticoats. Grancher in the middle with the men beating time and the ladies turning in a circle, then linking arms with the men.

A moment of silence when Proud Parry bowed to Miss Olson.

"Proud Parry hasn't danced in years," Gran hissed. "It's a white-haired teg that has bewitched him."

"Heisht, Mother," said Mrs. Tybach.

Twm watched fascinated as the fiddles soared and the Welsh harps twanged, as the drums beat while the people surged, laughing, clapping to the music . . . "She's staying, she's staying," said Twm over and over again to himself. "For Miss Olson I'll do better . . . I'll learn."

"Come on, Twm," called Gypsy. "Come on, let's go and look for my tribe."

"Not now, Gypsy," called Twm. "I'm going to dance with Miss Olson when Proud Parry's through."

When the music stopped, Twm brushed himself off and smoothed his hair down with spit. Then he walked right up to Miss Olson, and bowed like gentry. Miss Olson gave her lovely smile and said: "Twm, it will be a pleasure." They walked arm in arm into the dancing ring together.